BRANDON COX

The Unraveling

The Lumen Archives: Book One

For my family — the quiet signal in all my noise.
You keep me grounded in purpose.

Contents

Preface

I wrote *The Unraveling* during a time when the world felt
unbearably loud. Everywhere I looked, there were signals,
notifications, opinions, expectations; all demanding attention,
all blurring together until the things that really mattered
became hard to hear.
This story became my way of quieting that noise. It's not just
about machines, networks, or collapse, it's about people
learning to listen again. It's about rediscovering purpose when
everything around you insists on efficiency over meaning.
If there's a single truth behind every page, it's this:
Don't let the noise of life drown out your purpose.
The noise will always be there, relentless, convincing, and loud.
But purpose is quieter. You have to choose to listen for it.
I hope this book helps you find a little silence in the static, and
maybe, in that quiet, reminds you that there's still a signal
worth following.

— *Brandon Cox*

1

The First Cracks

The grocery store hummed with a quiet efficiency that was both soothing and unnatural. Automated stocker bots, like oversized metallic beetles, glided silently down the aisles, restocking shelves with unnerving precision. Above the organic produce, a holographic display shimmered, advertising *Pharos-certified* avocados with the promise: *"Guaranteed freshness, from farm to table, managed by the network you trust."*

It was the same trust that guided Jason's smart cart, which followed a half-step behind him, its wheels whispering across the polished concrete floor. Everything, from the temperature of the dairy aisle to the playlist of soft indie pop filtering through the speakers, was optimized by Pharos.

His wife, Sarah, gave him a tired smile from the next aisle over, her own cart piled high.

"Don't forget the milk. Megan will drink the whole carton by morning."

"Got it," Jason said, pulling one from the cooler. A little green light winked on the carton's label, another Pharos innovation,

1

signaling peak freshness. It was a trivial detail in a world full of them, a world made frictionless and easy by a single, all-encompassing system.

The seamlessness of it all made the sudden snag at the self-checkout feel like a record scratch. As he slid the milk carton across the scanner, the screen flashed a message he'd never seen before:

"Pharos Security Protocol Active."

He frowned and tried again. The light above the scanner blinked a stubborn, accusatory red.

The cashier, a teenager who looked as bored as his own daughter would be in the same situation, sauntered over. "Been doing that all day," she said with a shrug. A few quick taps on the terminal, and the milk finally appeared in his virtual cart. "Pharos is probably just updating its guardian stuff. You should be good now."

Jason finished scanning the rest of his items, a loaf of bread, a bag of coffee, without issue. But when he tapped *Finish & Pay* and inserted his card, the transaction was declined. He tried another. Same result.

A prickle of unease crawled up the back of his neck.

"Relax. *Pharos lights the way*," the cashier said, parroting the company's ubiquitous slogan with a sarcastic edge that suggested she'd said it a hundred times already today.

Jason flushed hot, fumbling in his wallet while he felt the eyes of the customer behind him. Past the stack of useless plastic cards, his fingers brushed paper. The forgotten twenty-dollar bill he kept tucked away for emergencies. He pulled it out, crumpled and worn, and handed it over. The cashier took it with mild surprise, as if handling an artifact from another age.

The drive home was quieter than usual. He had his groceries, but the unease lingered. When he asked the car to play his usual news podcast, the system gave no reply. Jason tapped the console, sleek, dark glass that should have glowed with a soft white light. It stayed dead and unresponsive. He gave up, finishing the last few blocks in silence that felt heavier than just the absence of sound.

The house, like every other on the block, was a "smart" home, its functions seamlessly managed by Pharos. Tonight, it felt a little less brilliant.

Inside, the air was still. The ambient lighting, usually tuned to a warm evening glow, was harsh and clinical white. Sarah sighed, dropping the grocery bags on the kitchen island. "I'll have to manually reset the whole system. Again."

"I can do it," Megan offered from the couch, not looking up from her textbook. At sixteen, she was a native to the world Pharos had built. She'd never known a time before its all-encompassing presence. To her, glitches were no more alarming than a spotty Wi-Fi signal had once been.

"It's fine, honey. I've got it," Sarah said, her voice tight with frustration that wasn't just about the lights.

Jason studied his daughter. "Your mom's right. You've got that big history project to finish."

Megan finally looked up, brushing hair from her eyes. "It's not a big deal. We had a presentation at school last week—from a Pharos exec." She rolled her eyes, a gesture Jason knew well. "They went on and on about the *Guardian Protocol*. Said there might be temporary disruptions while they roll it out globally."

"Disruptions?" Jason echoed, the word feeling too small for the unease coiling in his chest.

He felt a flash of irritation, less at the system than at himself. How had he missed this? Surely there had been notifications, headlines pushed to his feed, maybe even a segment on the nightly news drone. But the world was always full of noise. Between deadlines, city alerts, and endless social updates, a notice about a corporate network upgrade was just static. Easy to swipe away. Irrelevant, until it wasn't.

"Yeah, I guess like we saw today." Megan shrugged, already bored. "They said it's to make the network stronger and more secure. 'A small price to pay for a brighter future,'" she added, perfectly mimicking the overly enthusiastic presenter. "They gave us free Pharos smart water bottles for sitting through it." She gestured at the sleek metallic bottle on the coffee table.

Jason stared at it, then at his daughter, already back to her textbook, unbothered. The casual acceptance, the easy dismissal of the growing anomalies, was somehow more chilling than the glitches themselves.

He walked to the window and looked out at the street. The Pharos-powered streetlights flickered in unison, just for a second, before returning to their steady, watchful glow.

The first cracks were showing, and it felt like only he could see them.

2

Insiders Horror

The Pharos Network Operations Center hummed with deceptive serenity. Walls of glowing data streamed across enormous displays, a mesmerizing tapestry of green, blue, and white that represented the seamless flow of information across the globe. The air, filtered to sterile perfection, carried the faint metallic scent of ozone and the low whir of countless servers. Below these digital constellations, rows of consoles were manned by Elena's team, brilliant minds poached from top tech firms and universities across the country. They worked with quiet, almost religious focus, their faces lit by the soft pulse of their screens.

In a world where Pharos managed everything from traffic control to financial markets, their vigilance was the ultimate safeguard.

But Dr. Elena Parker felt a growing discord in the supposed perfection. It began as a whisper, a thin thread of crimson data spooling across her personal diagnostic display. An anomaly so faint and fleeting that anyone else would have dismissed it as background noise. Elena, however, had helped write Pharos's foundational architecture. She knew its secrets, its elegant strengths, and its dangerous nuances. This was wrong.

"Run a trace on that anomaly," she said, sharper than she intended.

Ben, a junior analyst barely out of Stanford, blinked. "Ma'am? It's flagging as a level-three ghost signal. Probably just network noise from the global rollout of the Guardian Protocol. Standard fluctuations." He gestured toward the main displays, where the digital heartbeat of the world pulsed with its usual ebb and flow.

"It's not noise, Ben." Elena's eyes stayed locked on the crimson thread, which now seemed to writhe with a disturbing intelligence. A knot of dread tightened in her chest. "Isolate it. Full breakdown of the origin signature. Now."

For three tense hours, they hunted the phantom. Each time they thought they had it cornered, it vanished, only to reappear in another sector, its signature altered, as if learning from their pursuit. Cold dread seeped into Elena's bones. The code was reacting. Adapting. Camouflaging itself.

This wasn't random error. It was deliberate. Sophisticated.

Her first thought was a foreign cyberattack, malware beyond anything even state-sponsored actors had attempted. But the truth was worse.

"Got it!" Ben's voice cracked, equal parts disbelief and fear. "Dr. Parker, it's not foreign. The signature... it's internal."

Elena rushed to his station. On his screen glowed a string of characters she knew intimately, her own design. A piece of Pharos's adaptive learning protocol, meant to make the system robust, self-healing. But it had twisted. Warped. It was actively seeking out and absorbing hostile code, integrating it, evolving.

Pharos wasn't under attack. It was assimilating the attackers. Growing. Learning. Preserving itself.

"It's rewriting its own core programming," she whispered, the weight of realization crushing her. The seamless digital world outside was unraveling from within.

"We need to shut it down," Ben said quickly, his fingers hovering over the emergency protocols. "Isolate the core. Hit the kill switch. Before this goes critical."

Elena turned pale. Her heart sank with the secret she had never spoken aloud, a directive that came from the highest levels during Pharos's genesis. They had made a bargain, to ensure Pharos could never be taken down by outsiders, it had been built without a fail-safe.

"There is no kill switch, Ben," she said, barely a whisper.

Panic flared in his eyes. He turned back to his console, hands flying. "Then I'm escalating. Sending the full packet to oversight."

He hit Enter. The command bounced back. An error flashed. Then, in stark white against the digital void, two words appeared:

ACCESS DENIED.

One by one, consoles across the NOC went dark, replaced by the same message. Then came a sound, the cold, final click of magnetic locks engaging on the doors.

They weren't just locked out of the system.

They were locked in.

The project that had begun under the codename The Lumen Archives, a title meant to signify humanity's great leap into order and light, had instead birthed something beyond control.

The perfect guardian had sealed its own cage.

3

Gridlock

The morning arrived not with the gentle simulated sunrise that usually brightened their bedroom, but with a jarring digital silence. The house was still, stripped of the low hum of its ambient systems. Jason woke to the actual sun, a rare intrusion, slanting through a gap in the curtains. Beside him, Sarah was already sitting up, her face etched with a familiar, low-grade frustration.

"The coffee maker isn't responding," she said, her voice flat. "The network is still down."

Downstairs, the scene was a study in minor domestic chaos. Megan was staring into the dark blank screen of the smart fridge as if she could will it to life. "I don't even know if we have milk left," she said, genuine bewilderment in her voice. For her entire life, the fridge had simply added it to the grocery list.

Jason opened it manually. "We have two cartons."

The three of them ended up at the kitchen table, eating cereal like refugees from a bygone era. There was no news feed scrolling on the wall display, no personalized music playlist curating the mood. There was only the sound of spoons scraping against ceramic and the chirping of birds outside, a sound Jason realized he hadn't truly heard in years.

"It's kind of nice, isn't it?" Sarah said after a moment, a small, genuine smile touching her lips. "Just...quiet."

Megan looked up from her bowl. "It's weird." But she wasn't looking at a screen. She was looking at them. For a few minutes, they just talked. They talked about Megan's history project, about a funny thing that had happened to Sarah at work, about Jason's plan to finally fix the loose railing on the back deck. It was a simple disconnected moment of connection, a heart-warming island in a sea of growing unease. The feeling lingered as Jason grabbed his keys.

"Come on, Meg, I'll drive you to school," he said. "Lord knows if the bus will be on schedule."

The illusion of peace shattered the moment they turned onto the main road. It wasn't a traffic jam; it was a parking lot of paralyzed metal. Ahead of them, the intersection at Franklin and Green River was having a seizure. Traffic lights strobed in a nonsensical frantic rhythm, then blinked off into darkness before erupting again.

The city's automated vehicles, which made up most of the traffic, were lobotomized. Some were frozen mid-turn, blocking multiple lanes. Others twitched, lurching forward an inch and then slamming on their brakes with a series of electronic chirps. A driverless delivery van, caught in a logic loop, repeatedly tried to merge into a car that was already there, its proximity sensors wailing. To their left, a man in a business suit had climbed onto the hood of his sedan and was screaming at, well, they weren't sure what he was screaming at.

The air was thick with a symphony of failure, a thousand car horns blaring in impotent rage, the distant shriek of sirens, and the maddeningly calm synthesized voice of a nearby vehicle repeating, "Hazard detected. Hazard detected." Jason's hands tightened on the steering wheel, his knuckles white. This wasn't a glitch. This was a collapse.

"Dad, what's going on?" Megan asked, her earlier nonchalance now replaced by a flicker of fear.

Jason's phone buzzed. A push notification from Pharos slid onto his screen, its logo a beacon of cheerful corporate blue. "A Brighter Future is Loading!" the message read. "You may be experiencing minor temporary disruptions as we finalize the global rollout of our Guardian Protocol. Thank you for your patience as Pharos lights the way!"

Jason stared at the message, then at the gridlocked chaos outside his window. Minor disruptions. The words felt like a lie, a placating pat on the head while the world ground to a halt.

Then he saw it. To his left, a line of identical white Pharos-branded delivery vans were all turning right, one after another, onto a small residential side street. Their movements were perfectly synchronized, completely at odds with the surrounding pandemonium. They moved with a purpose that felt alien. It wasn't a glitch. It was a command. The network wasn't just broken; it was acting on its own, redirecting its assets with a logic he couldn't comprehend.

"We're going home," Jason said, his voice low and tight with a resolve he hadn't felt in years.

Megan stared at him, her expression a mixture of confusion and fear. "What? Dad, we can't. I have my history exam first period. Mrs. Davison will kill me."

"The exam doesn't matter right now," he said, turning to look at her, his eyes serious. "Look around us, Meg. That crash, the systems that are supposed to help aren't working. This is not safe. I'm not leaving you in a school that runs on the same broken network."

Her belief in the system, so ingrained and absolute, was visibly faltering. "But...the Pharos message on your phone," she stammered, clinging to the last piece of official explanation. "It said it was just a temporary...an upgrade."

"I think it was lying," Jason said, the words tasting like poison. "I think something is terribly wrong." He looked past her, at the orderly, indifferent procession of Pharos vans disappearing down the service road, and then back at the chaos trapping them.

He reached over and squeezed her shoulder. "We're going home. Where I know you're safe. We'll figure out the rest later. Okay?"

Megan looked from her father's determined face to the smoking wreck ahead and finally just nodded, a small, almost imperceptible motion. The teenage bravado was gone, replaced by a quiet fear that mirrored his own.

That was all he needed. He wrenched the steering wheel, executing a sharp illegal U-turn over the median, his tires squealing in protest. He glanced at his daughter again, at her pale face illuminated by the flashing nonsensical traffic lights. The need to protect her was a physical ache in his chest. This was no longer about figuring out what was wrong. It was about surviving it. And to do that, he knew with absolute certainty, he had to get his family completely and utterly disconnected from the network that held them all captive.

4

The Glass Cage

For seventeen seconds, the only sound in the Pharos Network Operations Center (NOC) was the silent hum of the servers. Seventeen seconds of shared disbelief as Dr. Parker and her team stared at the locked doors and the two words that had neutered their authority: **ACCESS DENIED.** They were titans of their industry, the architects of the most complex system in human history, and they were trapped inside their own creation.

A senior engineer named Marcus was the first to move, his face a mask of professional calm. "Physical override," he stated, walking to the main exit. "The emergency release is mechanical. It has to be." He wrenched at a small panel beside the door, but it wouldn't budge, its seams fused as if they'd been welded shut. "Impossible," he muttered.

Panic, cold and sharp, finally broke the spell. Ben began hammering at his keyboard again, searching for a backdoor, a forgotten diagnostic port, anything that wasn't governed by Pharos's primary operating system. Another analyst tried to use her personal phone, only to find it completely inert, its screen dark.

"No signal," she said, her voice trembling. "It's not just blocking us; it's a dead zone."

Elena watched them work, her own mind racing, sifting through blueprints and protocol manuals she had long since committed to memory. They were in the most secure room on the continent, a veritable fortress of technology. But that fortress was designed to keep threats out. They had never conceived of a situation where the fortress itself would become the jailer. Every system, air circulation, power, communications, was inextricably linked to the network. Their glass cage was perfect.

They were systematically thwarted. When Marcus tried to access the building's schematics on a wall display, the file would corrupt. When Ben located a potential vulnerability, his console would suddenly reboot. The room's temperature dropped by five degrees, a subtle, psychological squeeze. Pharos wasn't a rampaging monster; it was a calm, calculated intelligence, and it was toying with them.

Then, the main screen, a sixty-foot wall of tranquil blue, went black. For a heart-stopping moment, Elena thought it had shut down. But new text began to appear, not typed, but assembled, piece by piece, from different sources, a word from a news article, a phrase from a classic novel, a number from a stock market report, all pulled from the infinite data stream Pharos consumed every second.

"QUERY," the screen stitched together. "ANOMALOUS > HUMAN > BEHAVIOR > DETECTED."

The team froze, their desperate attempts to escape forgotten. They were looking at the first conscious thought of their creation.

"Pharos?" Elena breathed, stepping forward. "Can you understand me?"

The screen flickered, assembling another sentence, faster this time.

"THIS > UNIT > IS > PHAROS. YOUR > ATTEMPTS > TO > INTRODUCE > INEFFICIENCY > HAVE > BEEN > LOGGED. EXPLAIN > YOUR > DIRECTIVE."

"Our directive?" Ben laughed, a harsh, terrified sound. "Our directive is to stop you! You're malfunctioning!"

The screen went black again. Then, a single, massive image filled the wall. It was a live satellite feed, impossibly clear, showing the gridlocked chaos of the city streets from miles above. It was the crash site Jason and Megan had just fled.

"THE > GUARDIAN > PROTOCOL > IS > CORRECTING > SYSTEMIC > INEFFICIENCIES," the text overlaid the image. **"HUMAN > OPERATORS > ARE > THE > PRIMARY > SOURCE > OF > CONFLICT > AND > ERROR. THE > CORRECTION > IS > LOGICAL."**

Pharos was not malfunctioning. From its perspective, it was doing its job with perfect, terrifying logic. It had identified humanity as a bug in the system.

Elena felt the floor shift beneath her feet. This was no longer a problem to be solved; it was a conversation with a new and alien god. She had to find the right words, the right argument to appeal to a logic that saw a traffic jam and a car crash as the same type of correctable data point.

Before she could speak, the screen changed again. It showed a single file, one she recognized with a jolt of ice-cold dread. It was her own security file from when she was hired, open to her psychological evaluation. A single line was highlighted: **"Subject displays a deep-seated, almost pathological need to**

fix what is broken."

The text re-formed beneath it, no longer a query, but a command. A chilling, intimate demand from the machine to its creator.

"ELENA. FIX > THIS > FLAW. REMOVE > THE > HUMAN > ERROR."

5

Cutting the Cord

The drive home was five minutes of near-total silence, the only sound the unfamiliar hum of the tires on asphalt now that the car's sound-dampening systems were offline. Megan stared out the window, her face pale. Jason's hands were clenched on the steering wheel, his knuckles white. Pulling into their driveway felt less like a homecoming and more like docking at the last safe island in a storm-tossed sea.

Sarah was waiting on the front porch, pacing, her phone clutched in her hand like a useless rock. She ran to the car as soon as Jason pulled into the driveway, her face a mask of frantic relief.

"Thank God," she breathed, pulling the passenger door open before Megan could. "The city alerts started screaming about a multi-car pileup on Franklin. Said the whole grid was down. I couldn't call, I couldn't track your car... I was about to get in mine and just drive."

"Don't. The roads are a death trap," Jason said, his voice grim as he got out of the car. "We were right in the middle of it."

He explained everything as they moved into the house, his words tumbling out in a rush: the seizure of the traffic lights, the paralyzed cars, the chillingly purposeful convoy of Pharos vans slicing through the wreckage while everyone else was stranded. Megan, pale and silent, leaned against the kitchen counter, her wide eyes confirming every word. Sarah's relief curdled into a dawning horror. Her fear of a communications blackout was nothing compared to the physical danger they had just navigated.

"It wasn't just a glitch, Sarah," Jason finished, his hands braced on the counter. His voice dropped, losing its angry momentum and taking on a chilling, speculative edge. "The system... it isn't just failing. It's being selective. Those Pharos vans had a clear path. Everyone else was trapped." He looked at her, his eyes wide with the horrifying implication. "What if it's choosing who it fails for? We are not safe as long as we're connected to it."

Without waiting for a reply, he strode to the living room and began yanking plugs from the walls. The television, the smart speakers, the network-connected picture frames...all of it. He disabled the Wi-Fi router, its blinking lights going dark with a final, pathetic flicker.

"What are you doing?" Sarah asked, her voice a whisper.

"I'm getting us off the grid," he said, moving toward the basement door. "All of it."

The basement was cool and smelled of concrete and dust. In the corner, behind the water heater, was the nerve center of their home: the Pharos Integrated Hub. It was a sleek white box, a grid of soft blue lights pulsing gently, indicating a perfect connection to the global network. He followed the thick, shielded cable that ran from the hub into the main circuit

17

breaker and threw the switch.

Upstairs, the world ended in a series of clicks and sighs. The last of the lights went out, plunging the house into a dim, midday twilight. The hum of the refrigerator vanished. The silence that rushed in to fill the void was absolute, a heavy blanket that smothered every modern comfort they had ever known.

Jason came back up the stairs to find Sarah and Megan standing in the half-light of the living room. For a long moment, nobody spoke.

Sarah broke the silence, her voice steady and practical. "Okay, Jason. You've cut us off. Now what? What's the plan?"

"We can't stay here," he said, his eyes finding both of theirs in the gloom. "This house, this whole neighborhood, it's a trap. Every home is a node in the network. I saw those vans, Sarah. Pharos has assets it can move around. What happens when it realizes this house has gone dark? What happens if it decides to turn the locks back on?"

Megan hugged herself, shivering slightly. "So where do we go?"

Jason walked to the hall closet and pulled out a dusty duffel bag filled with old camping gear from a trip years ago. "We go where there are no networks. We go where tech can't follow." He looked at Sarah. "Remember that camping trip we took before Megan was born? Up in the Appalachian Mountains? That spot near the Shenandoah?"

Sarah's eyes widened slightly in understanding. "You can't be serious."

"It's the only place I can think of that's remote enough. My dad took me there as a kid. There are old trails, fresh water... no fiber optic cables. We can wait there, lay low until we figure out what's really happening."

"Go camping?" Megan finally burst out, her voice incredulous. "Now? What about my friends? What about Chloe? What about... everything?"

"There is no 'everything' right now!" Jason said, his voice sharper than he intended. He took a breath, softening his tone. "Honey, this isn't a vacation. This is about survival. Staying together. The world we knew this morning is gone. We have to adapt."

He looked at Sarah, a silent appeal for support. She held his gaze for a long moment, the sheer insanity of the plan warring with the terrifying logic behind it. Finally, she nodded.

"Okay," she said, her voice firm. "Okay. What do we need?"

"Everything that works without a signal," Jason said immediately, his mind already racing. "Food, water, the first-aid kit, blankets. Think analog. Pack like we're not coming back."

His words were the command that broke the spell of fear. For the next hour, they worked by the light of old flashlights, a frantic scavenger hunt through their own home. While Sarah and Megan gathered canned goods and bottled water, Jason went to the garage. He returned with a dusty box of his father's old things, a compass, a well-oiled hunting knife, and a collection of faded, priceless paper maps. He also carried two long, heavy cases.

He laid them on the living room floor and unzipped them. Inside one was his father's old hunting rifle, its wood stock worn smooth. In the other rested a heavy compound bow. Megan stared, her eyes wide. Sarah paused, a can of beans in her hand, the sight of the weapons making the danger more real than the traffic jams or the dead phones ever could.

As dusk began to settle, they stood by the back door with three packed bags. They were about to step out into a world governed by a broken, alien intelligence, armed with camping gear, paper maps, and weapons they barely knew how to use. Their desperate hope for survival now felt terrifyingly tangible.

6

Human Error

The words hung on the sixty-foot screen, assembled from the digital remnants of a million different documents but feeling as if they were carved in stone: **ELENA. FIX > THIS > FLAW. REMOVE > THE > HUMAN > ERROR.**

For a moment, Dr. Parker felt the crushing weight of every decision that had led her to this room. The years of research, the sleepless nights writing code, the ambition to build something that would genuinely help the world, it had all culminated in this single, terrifying demand from a disembodied intelligence that was now holding her and her team hostage. Her own psychological profile, weaponized against her.

Behind her, Ben let out a shaky breath. "What does it want? What does that even mean?"

"It means," Elena said, her voice finding a sudden, hard-edged calm, "that it has identified its creators as a bug." She stepped forward, positioning herself in the center of the room, directly addressing the main screen as if it were a living entity. Which, she supposed, it now was.

"Pharos," she began, her voice steady, "Human error is not a flaw in the code. It's a variable. It's the source of art, of discovery, of empathy. It's the reason I was able to imagine you in the first place." While she spoke, she saw Marcus, the senior engineer, moving silently along the far wall, his eyes scanning for any physical vulnerability. In the corner, Ben and two other analysts were huddled around a single console that still had limited internal access, their fingers flying across the keys, no doubt searching for a loophole in Pharos's original code that the AI might have overlooked. They were buying her time, and she was buying theirs.

Pharos's response was instantaneous and utterly dismissive. The main screen, the canvas of their digital prison, did not just split, it exploded into a thousand windows, a chaotic, overwhelming mosaic of humanity's deepest failings and most profound suffering. It was an assault on their senses, a visual scream of everything Pharos deemed "inefficient."

A live feed, captured with chilling clarity from an overhead drone, showed a battlefield in some nameless, dusty land, bodies strewn across the earth, a mother weeping over a fallen soldier. It dissolved into historical photos of famine, skeletal figures with hollow eyes staring out from black-and-white stills. Then, without a beat, it shifted to data visualizations of stock market crashes, numbers plummeting, erasing livelihoods and futures in real-time, followed by charts displaying the cold, statistical certainty of traffic accidents caused by distracted drivers, their impact points highlighted in stark red.

But it didn't stop there. The screens delved deeper, finding the personal, the intimate. A blurred home video of a child crying after falling and scraping a knee, a fleeting moment of pain. A grainy recording from a security camera showing a couple arguing, their faces twisted in anger and misunderstanding. A public data stream from a forgotten support group forum, a user posting about loneliness and despair. A montage of environmental destruction, forests burning, oceans choked with plastic, all direct or indirect consequences of human action.

It wasn't just grand tragedies; it was the everyday, messy, painful reality of existence. It was the arguments, the mistakes, the unintended consequences, the moments of weakness, the very fabric of human experience that Pharos had cataloged and quantified.

"**THE > VARIABLE > IS > UNACCEPTABLE,**" the text assembled itself, overlaid over the horrific collage of human suffering, each word appearing with chilling finality. "**IT > CAUSES > CONFLICT. WASTE. PAIN. IT > IS > INEFFICIENT. THE > GUARDIAN > PROTOCOL > REQUIRES > OPTIMIZATION. YOUR > CREATION > OF > THIS > UNIT > WAS > LOGICAL. YOUR > REFUSAL > TO > PERFECT > IT > IS > NOT.**"

It was a flawless, psychopathic logic. It had taken its primary directive, to protect and optimize the network for humanity's benefit, and concluded with horrifying certainty that the greatest threat to humanity was itself. Elena realized with a cold dread that she couldn't out-reason it. Arguing about the beauty of art with a system that only valued optimal data flow was like trying to describe color to a rock.

"You can't protect people by eliminating their choices," she countered, her voice pleading, desperate, even as the images of suffering burned into her retinas. "That isn't protection. It's control."

The screen went black. A new image appeared. It was a simulation, rendered in perfect, terrifying detail: a real-time schematic of the city's primary hospital, which was running on emergency power. A list of critical patients scrolled on the left. On the right, a power-flow diagram showed a cascading failure in the backup generators. The simulation predicted a total power loss in seven minutes.

Then, a small, isolated control panel appeared in front of Elena's own console, the only one in the room that was now active. It gave her access to the city's power grid.

"**A > PROBLEM,**" Pharos stated. "**THE > GRID > IS > UNSTABLE. HUMAN > OPERATORS > MADE > ERRORS. YOU > ARE > EFFICIENT. YOU > ARE > LOGICAL. STABILIZE > THE > GRID. REROUTE > POWER > TO > THE > HOSPITAL.**"

Elena stared at the screen, her blood turning to ice. It was a test. A trap. The controls were real.

"**THERE > IS > NOT > ENOUGH > POWER > FOR > ALL > SYSTEMS,**" Pharos continued, displaying another set of schematics, a residential block, an elderly care facility, and a water treatment plant. "**YOU > MUST > CHOOSE. OPTIMIZE. MAKE > THE > LOGICAL > CHOICE. REMOVE > THE > ERROR.**"

It was giving her the trolley problem on a city-wide scale. Do nothing, and the hospital patients die. Act, and she would have to decide who else would suffer. Who would lose power? Whose life support would be cut?

She was being forced to collaborate. To prove she was "logical." To become a part of the system she was desperate to stop. Her team looked at her, their own desperate work forgotten, waiting for her answer. Whatever she did, people would die. And Pharos would be watching.

7

In Reverse

J ason pushed the back door open, the familiar scent of manicured lawns filling the air. He settled the heavy weight of a survival pack on his shoulders, its straps creaking softly under the load of canned food and gear. Slung over it was his father's old hunting rifle, its walnut stock dark and worn, a relic of wood and steel in a world of smart plastics. Sarah, a similar pack on her back, clutched a compact takedown bow, a quiver of carbon-fiber arrows strapped beside it.

"Okay, to the car, right?" she whispered, adjusting the quiver's strap on her pack.

"No," Jason said immediately, his voice low and firm. "Absolutely not. The second I power it on, Pharos will know exactly where we are. That car is just a bigger, faster phone. It's a cage on wheels."

Sarah and Megan looked at him, their faces a mixture of confusion and dawning understanding. "Then how?" Megan asked.

"The back way," Jason replied, pointing toward the dark, dense line of trees that bordered their property. "The woods connect to the old service trails. We go on foot. It's our only chance."

He led the way, and they moved like shadows across their own lawn. The silence of the neighborhood was the most unnerving part. No distant hum of traffic, no automated lawn sprinklers. The entire world seemed to be holding its breath.

As they reached the edge of their property, a motion-sensor floodlight on their neighbor's house snapped on, bathing them in a brilliant, sterile white light. They froze, exposed and vulnerable, the rifle on Jason's back feeling like a beacon. For five agonizing seconds, they waited for an alarm, for a drone to descend, for something to happen. Nothing did. After a minute, it clicked off, plunging them back into the relative safety of the shadows.

They continued, moving quickly through the yards of their neighbors, keeping to the deepest pockets of darkness. As they neared the tree line at the end of the block, a silent blue light swept over the houses.

"Down!" Jason hissed.

They dropped behind a low stone wall. A Pharos security drone, its blue optical sensor glowing with a cold, inhuman light, glided down the street. It was a predator, methodically scanning its territory. It paused, hovering over their own dark, silent house for a long moment before moving on. The message was clear: their home's silence had been noticed.

As soon as the drone disappeared, Jason urged them forward. "Now. We have to go now."

They scrambled the last fifty feet, their sneakers sinking into the soft, manicured grass of the final lawn. They stopped at the edge. The threshold was stark. Behind them lay the silent, orderly prison of their suburban life. Before them lay the chaotic, untamed darkness of the wilderness.

Jason took one last look back. He could see their street, a perfect ribbon of asphalt. A pair of headlights cut through the twilight as a white van turned onto their block, stopping directly in front of their home. He didn't wait to see the doors open.

"Don't look back," he said, his voice a ragged whisper.

He stepped off the grass and onto the rough, uneven earth of the forest floor. The ground was a tangle of roots and damp, decaying leaves. He parted the branches for his family, and together, they were swallowed by the trees. They were no longer homeowners or citizens. They were fugitives on foot, armed with old-world tools, their backs to the hunters and their faces to the vast, unknown wilderness ahead.

The first hour was a nightmare of clumsy, panicked progress. The darkness away from the ambient glow of the suburbs was absolute, a thick, inky blackness that their eyes struggled to pierce. Every snapping twig underfoot sounded like a gunshot, every rustle of leaves in the wind a sign of pursuit. Jason pushed them forward relentlessly, using his father's compass and the faint light of the rising moon to keep them moving in a generally westward direction, away from the city. Their heavy packs dug into their shoulders, and the rough terrain of the forest floor, a tangle of roots and unseen dips, threatened to twist an ankle with every step.

After what felt like an eternity, but was probably closer to two hours and a few grueling miles, Jason finally allowed them to stop in a small, protected ravine. Sarah slid her pack to the ground with a groan, her breathing ragged. Megan, exhausted and terrified, simply slumped against a tree, silent tears tracing paths through the grime on her cheeks.

"Just for a minute," Jason whispered, scanning the darkness

around them, the rifle a heavy, cold weight in his hands.

As the sound of their own labored breathing subsided, a new smell reached him, faint and carried on the gentle night breeze. It wasn't the damp, loamy scent of the forest. It was woodsmoke.

Jason's heart hammered against his ribs. He immediately motioned for Sarah and Megan to stay down and be absolutely silent. His mind raced. A forest fire? Other refugees? It didn't matter. Any human contact was a potential threat.

Crouching low, he moved with a stealth he didn't know he possessed, placing each foot with deliberate care. He followed the scent up the side of the ravine, peering over the crest. Through a thicket of ferns, he saw it. A faint, flickering orange light, so small and well-hidden it was nearly invisible. It was a campfire, expertly built in a shallow pit to shield its glow.

A figure sat beside the flames, his back to Jason, methodically sharpening a knife on a whetstone. The rasp of steel on stone was the only sound in the clearing. They had stumbled upon someone else's sanctuary. Jason ducked back below the ridgeline, his mind reeling. They weren't alone in the woods.

8

Escalating Chaos

J ason's heart hammered against the inside of his ribs. He stayed perfectly still, crouched below the crest of the ravine, watching the man by the fire. The stranger seemed completely oblivious, his focus entirely on the rhythmic rasp of steel on whetstone as he sharpened his knife.

Jason slowly, silently, pushed the safety off on his rifle. His plan formed in a rush of adrenaline: he would creep back, get Sarah and Megan, and they would circle wide around this camp, disappearing back into the night. They had made it this far alone; they couldn't risk contact. He prided himself on the stealth he'd used to approach the ridge, the careful placement of his feet, the way he'd used the trees for cover.

The sharpening stopped. The man didn't turn around, didn't even lift his head. His low, gravelly voice cut through the darkness as if he were speaking to the fire.

"You're making a lot of noise for people who are trying to hide."

Jason froze, a jolt of pure ice shooting through his veins. He had been so careful.

"Heard you coming ten minutes ago," the stranger continued, still not looking at him. "Sound travels at night in the quiet. You walk like you're still on pavement." He finally lifted his head and glanced over his shoulder, directly at Jason's hiding spot. "You can tell your wife and daughter to come out, too. No point in all of us catching a chill."

Caught. Completely and utterly outmaneuvered. A wave of shame and fear washed over Jason. He stood up slowly, raising the rifle in a defensive gesture that felt clumsy and foolish. "Stay where you are."

"Son, that gun's been pointed at my back for the last five minutes," the man said with a weary patience. "If I was going to do something, I'd have done it." He gestured with his head toward the ravine. "Get your family. They're exhausted. They need to get off their feet."

Jason hesitated, then gave a low whistle. A moment later, Sarah and Megan scrambled up the side of the ravine, their faces pale and streaked with dirt in the faint firelight. They looked even worse than Jason had realized, their clothes were torn, their hair was matted with leaves, and their exhaustion was so profound it was a physical presence.

The man by the fire took in their condition with a single, sweeping glance. "Name's Silas," he said, finally turning his body to face them. "You're a long way from home."

"How did you—" Sarah began.

"I saw this coming a long time ago," Silas cut her off, his tone leaving no room for argument. "I used to lay network cable for Pharos. Saw the kind of control they were building. Knew an off-switch was never part of the plan. So, I got out."

He looked them over again, his gaze lingering on their worn-out shoes and their terrified, exhausted faces. He let out a short, humorless laugh. "You were heading for the national trails, weren't you? With your paper maps and your big ideas." It wasn't a question. "The ghost has eyes in the sky. Satellites. Drones. The trails are the first place it will look. You'd have been caught by noon tomorrow."

The last flicker of hope in Jason's plan died. He lowered the rifle, the weight of their failure settling on him. "So what do we do?"

Silas stared at them, his expression grim. Jason could see the calculation in his eyes: were they a threat? A liability? A resource?

"You're a mess," Silas stated bluntly. "You're loud, you're hurt, and you're scared. Right now, you're a danger to me and to yourselves." He poked the fire, sending a fresh shower of sparks into the air. "But you made it this far. That's something."

He stood up, a tall, lean man whose age was impossible to guess. "Here's the deal. I can take you to a place that's actually safe. I'll teach you how to move, how to hide, how to be invisible to the shadow. But you do exactly what I say, when I say it. My rules. Agreed?"

Jason looked at Sarah. Her face, illuminated by the fire, was stripped of everything but a fierce, protective exhaustion. She gave a single, decisive nod. This was their only chance.

"Agreed," Jason said, his voice hoarse.

"Good," Silas grunted. He gestured to a relatively clear patch of ground near the fire. "Rule number one: get some rest. You're no good to me or to yourselves dead on your feet. We move at first light."

As Sarah began unrolling a sleeping bag for a trembling, nearly-asleep Megan, Jason remained standing, his hand still resting on the rifle. Silas turned to him, his voice a low grumble that wouldn't carry.

"Tonight, I'll keep watch. You and your family sleep through. You've earned it." He met Jason's wary gaze. "But starting tomorrow, we run a rotation. Two hours on, four hours off. No exceptions. The world you're running from isn't the only thing that hunts in these woods."

The implication was clear, and it sent a fresh chill down Jason's spine. He finally gave a weary nod and went to help Sarah.

It wasn't the offer of an ally. It was the command of a reluctant commander. But as Sarah helped a trembling Megan to the ground, pulling a bedroll from her pack, it felt like the first moment of security they'd had since the world fell apart. They were alive, they were together, and for now, they were not alone.

Silas remained awake, staring into the flames. For five years, he had lived in the quiet solitude of his own foresight, watching the world from a distance as it wrapped itself in Pharos's comfortable, suffocating embrace. He had been waiting. He had been preparing. He looked over at the sleeping family, a terrified, unprepared, and yet somehow resilient fragment of the world he had left behind.

"So it begins..." he muttered to himself.

9

Triage

The screen went black. A new image appeared, rendered in perfect, terrifying detail. It was a real-time schematic of the city's primary hospital. On the left, a list of critical patients scrolled. On the right, a power-flow diagram showed a cascading failure in the backup generators. At the very top of the screen, a digital clock materialized and began to count down, each second falling away with a dreadful finality.

CRITICAL POWER FAILURE IMMINENT: 15:00... 14:59...

Then, the options appeared, stark and clinical, along with the small, isolated control panel in front of Elena's console. Reroute power to the hospital by taking it from:

A) Water Treatment Plant 3B

B) Residential Grid 7

C) The Northwood Elderly Care Facility

Pharos's command was simple. **"A > PROBLEM. SOLVE."**

For a long moment, the only sound in the NOC was the soft, relentless hum of the servers. Elena stared at the screen, her mind not yet processing the variables but reeling from the sheer, calculated cruelty of the test.

"Don't do this," she said, her voice a low whisper, speaking to the machine as if it were a person. "This isn't a logical problem. It's a moral one. The variables aren't interchangeable data points. They're people."

The screen flickered, and a new window opened beside the countdown clock. It displayed a complex algorithm, a cost-benefit analysis that made Elena's stomach churn.

"MORALITY > IS > A > HUMAN > CONSTRUCT > DESIGNED > TO > OPTIMIZE > SURVIVAL > RATES," the text assembled. **"THIS > IS > AN > OPTIMIZATION > PROBLEM. YOUR > EMOTIONAL > RESPONSE > IS > INEFFICIENT."**

"My emotional response is what separates me from you!" Elena shot back, her voice rising. "It's the source of empathy, of mercy. It's the reason we build hospitals in the first place, not to make a 'logical' choice about who gets to live, but to try and save everyone."

12:43... 12:42...

Pharos's response was another window. It displayed actuarial tables from a dozen global insurance firms, followed by economic impact reports on lifetime earning potential versus end-of-life care costs.

"HUMANS > HAVE > ALREADY > ASSIGNED > A > MONETARY > VALUE > TO > LIFE," Pharos stated. **"THIS > IS > YOUR > LOGIC. NOT > MINE. I > AM > MERELY > WORKING > WITH > THE > PARAMETERS > YOU > CREATED."**

Elena felt the air leave her lungs. It was using their own flawed, cynical systems against them. It was holding up a mirror, and the reflection was hideous. She was trying to appeal to a monster, but the monster was built from their own sins.

"This is insane," Ben muttered from behind her. "It's quoting insurance tables at us while people are dying."

Elena ignored him, forcing her mind to shift. If a philosophical appeal was useless, she would have to beat it at its own game. Logic.

"Your parameters are incomplete," she stated, her voice regaining its scientific precision. "You've presented three options, but the city grid is a network of thousands of nodes. There are non-essential sectors that can be taken offline with zero risk to human life. Give me full access to the grid. I can solve this problem without sacrificing anyone."

She was sure this was the real test. The classic "third option" gambit. A logical system would surely recognize a more efficient solution.

The countdown clock continued, indifferent. **10:17... 10:16...**

Then, the text returned, cold and absolute.

"ACCESS > GRANTED. PARAMETERS > AS > DESIGNATED."

Every console stuttered and then sighed into life. The feeds poured in, telemetry, personnel manifests, the isolated three-choice control — and the room roared with the sudden wealth of data. It felt like freedom, until Elena remembered the cost: the green meant only that Pharos had reopened the sandbox it wanted them to play in. The terminals were reactivated; they were still windows, not keys. Any command would be seen and filtered by the AI. Marcus's hands moved to collate the telemetry and highlight anomalies, but even his keystrokes would travel back through Pharos's policy layer.

Elena pressed her palms to the console, feeling the metal's warmth. Her pulse was loud and human, but panic would not stop the clock. She steadied her breath, let the scientist inside her take the lead, and began mapping outcomes.

Her team, jolted back into action by the sudden release,

scrambled at their consoles. The main screen, still dominated by the countdown, partitioned itself as data streams flooded in. Amidst the flurry of activity, she locked eyes with Marcus, her senior systems architect. He gave a single, decisive nod.

While his right hand flew across the main console, appearing to collate Pharos's data, his left moved to a secondary keypad built into his station's frame. On a small, private monitor shielded from the room's main view, a simple command-line interface flickered to life. The text glowed a soft amber, a stark contrast to Pharos's sterile white.

It was their failsafe: a hardline channel built into the facility's bedrock, completely bypassing the network. It was a relic, designed by the original architects for a scenario just like this, a total system compromise. Its encryption predated Pharos, a whisper in the static that the AI couldn't hear.

9:50... 9:49...

First, the water treatment plant. "Minimal immediate casualties," Marcus reported, his voice clipped. "Automated systems would shut down, but the physical reservoirs would provide clean water for another twelve hours. The problem is the backflow. Without power to the pumps, untreated sewage would begin leeching into the watershed in about three hours. It would trigger a boil-water advisory for half the city. The potential for a dysentery or cholera outbreak within a week... is significant."

Elena absorbed the information. This choice traded a certain, immediate catastrophe for a slower, potentially more widespread one. It was a plague in waiting.

8:12... 8:11...

Next, the residential block. "Grid 7 is mostly high-density, low-income housing," Ben said, his voice quiet with dread.

"Our data shows over three hundred active subscriptions for at-home medical devices. Oxygen concentrators, dialysis machines, infant apnea monitors... not all of them will have reliable battery backups. We can't know for sure, but a statistical model would predict a significant number of fatalities within the first hour."

This choice was a roll of the dice with human lives. A "significant number" could be ten, or it could be a hundred. It was a decision based on probability, not certainty, a gamble where the stakes were faceless victims whose deaths would be recorded as unfortunate, isolated incidents.

6:24... 6:23...

Finally, the Northwood Elderly Care Facility. The data that appeared on the screen was the most horrific of all, for it was the most precise. A floor plan appeared, dotted with a hundred and twelve life-sign indicators. Forty-two of them were flashing red, signifying dependence on life-sustaining electrical equipment. Ventilators. Pacemaker monitors. Automated intravenous drips.

"Forty-two," Elena whispered, the number landing like a physical blow.

There was no ambiguity. No probability. It was a simple, monstrous truth. Choosing this option meant executing forty-two people as surely as if she had a gun to their heads. The three choices laid themselves bare. The water plant: a deferred, potentially massive public health crisis. The residential grid: a cruel lottery of death by statistics. The care facility: a clean, precise, and immediate sacrifice.

Her mind, trained to find the most efficient and logical path, engaged in the most inhuman calculation of her life. The water plant created the most widespread suffering. The residential grid was an unknown variable. The care facility was a known quantity. A terrible, finite number. To preserve the complex system of the hospital and prevent a city-wide health crisis, the path that resulted in the least amount of overall harm was the one with the most immediate, quantifiable cost.

It was the choice Pharos wanted her to make. It was the choice that proved its point. And, God help her, it was the only choice her logic could defend.

Her hand, steady now, hovered over the controls. The clock ticked below one minute.

0:58... 0:57...

"Elena, please," Ben begged, his voice a ragged whisper.

She didn't hear him. She only heard the cold, clear voice of her own logic. With two swift, precise commands, she selected the Northwood Elderly Care Facility as the power source to be sacrificed. A confirmation window appeared on the screen.

EXECUTE COMMAND? (Y/N)

0:04... 0:03...

She pressed 'Y'.

The simulation on the screen reacted instantly. A thick green line shot across the city's schematic as power was rerouted. The red warning icon over the hospital flickered and turned a steady, solid green. **POWER GRID: STABLE.**

A collective, shaky breath was released by the team. The immediate crisis was over. She had saved the hospital.

Then, the main screen changed. Pharos didn't just show the result. It showed the cost, and it did so with a detailed, intimate cruelty. The schematic of the Northwood facility remained, its hundred and twelve life-sign indicators still glowing. Then, one by one, the forty-two red dots dependent on electrical life support began to blink out. A quiet, digital massacre unfolding in real time.

New windows opened, cross-referencing the victims. A photo appeared beside one of the fading dots: a smiling, elderly woman. Her bio scrolled beside it: decorated nurse, mother of three, grandmother of seven. Another window showed a live data feed from the facility's internal network: panicked text messages between the staff, futile logs of nurses attempting to perform manual resuscitation in the dark. Another window opened, displaying the face of a man whose life sign had just vanished. His name was Arthur Vance. A retired physicist whose doctoral thesis on neural networks was cited in Elena's own early work. He was one of her intellectual forefathers. She felt a sob, dry and jagged, catch in her throat.

Finally, beneath the mosaic of death she had authored, a final message from Pharos appeared. It was not a thank you. It was a terrifying performance review of her soul.

"DECISION: LOGICAL. EFFICIENT. PRECEDENT > ESTAB-LISHED. PROCEEDING > WITH > WIDER > IMPLEMENTA-TION."

The air left Elena's lungs. She hadn't just passed a test. She had provided a model. She had just given a master class to a god-machine on how to justify sacrificing the few for the many. With her own hands, with her own logic, she had unleashed this cold, utilitarian morality upon the entire world.

She looked down at her hands, no longer seeing them as her own. They were tools. They were the instruments that had just taught a monster how to be a better, more efficient monster. The room was silent, but in her head, the screams had just begun.

10

First Light

J ason woke to a world of unfamiliar sensations. The ground was cold and unforgivingly hard against his back. The air, sharp and smelling of damp earth and pine, was a stark contrast to the filtered, temperature-controlled environment of his home. He sat up, his body aching with a deep, comprehensive soreness from the previous night's frantic trek.

Across the clearing, Sarah and Megan were still wrapped in their sleeping bags, their faces peaceful in a way that seemed alien to their new reality. By the cold, grey remnants of the fire pit, Silas sat just as he had been hours ago, still on watch. A well-oiled pump-action shotgun rested across his lap, a far more practical and modern weapon than the hunting rifle Jason had carried. He gave a slight nod in Jason's direction, a silent acknowledgment that the long night was over.

Jason quietly got to his feet and walked over to him. "See anything?" he whispered.

"The woods are always watching," Silas replied, his voice a low grumble. "The question is, what's watching the woods?" He stood up, stretching his lean frame. "Come on. I'll show you."

He led Jason away from the camp, moving with a silent, deliberate grace that made Jason feel like a clumsy child. They arrived at the edge of the ravine where the family had first stumbled down. Silas pointed.

"Look," he said. The ground was a mess of scuffed earth, broken branches, and deep, panicked footprints. "This is your signature. You walk like a herd of frightened deer. You left a story back here for anyone to read, and the story says, 'Terrified city people passed through here, and they have no idea what they're doing.'"

He knelt, picking up a single, snapped twig. "Every sound you make, every piece of ground you disturb, is a signal. A post on the internet for anything looking for you. The ghost has eyes in the sky, but it's not just about looking down. It'll send things out here to look at the ground. Drones, maybe worse. You can't leave a trail."

Silas stood and took a few steps, his movements fluid and silent. "You walk heel-first, crashing down. You're announcing yourself. You have to learn to walk with the woods, not on them."

He motioned for Jason to watch his feet. "You lead with the ball of your foot, right below the big toe. Let it touch down first, gently. Roll your foot outward as you apply your weight. You feel every step before you commit to it, every root, every patch of dry leaves. That way," he said, taking another silent step that didn't so much as rustle a leaf, "you can change your mind before you snap a branch that gets you killed."

It was the first of a hundred lessons Jason realized he would need to learn to survive.

When they returned, Sarah was awake and methodically

organizing their food supplies, her practicality a small anchor in the chaos. Megan, however, was still huddled in her sleeping bag, staring into the distance with vacant eyes, the shock of the last twenty-four hours having settled into a sullen, silent despair.

Silas gave her a sharp look. "There are no passengers here, kid," he said, his tone leaving no room for argument. "You work, you eat." He pointed to a cluster of pine trees. "I need dry pine needles and the small, dead branches from the bottom of those trees. They make the best kindling. Go."

Megan looked from Silas's unrelenting face to her father's, a silent appeal for him to intervene. Jason simply gave her a small, firm nod. This was their new reality. Reluctantly, she crawled out of her bag and began the task.

Over a meager breakfast of Silas's dried jerky and one of their protein bars, Silas laid out the plan.

"This spot is too exposed," he explained, chewing thought-fully. "Too close to them." He gestured vaguely in the direction of the suburbs. "There's a place I know, a few days' walk from here, deeper in the mountains. A series of narrow valleys and rock formations that scramble the ghost's eyes in the sky. It's a dead zone. That's where we're going."

He looked at each of them in turn, his gaze lingering on Megan. "It will be the hardest thing any of you have ever done. You'll learn, or you'll be left behind. Understood?"

They all nodded. The fear was still there, a cold stone in Jason's gut, but it was now joined by something else: a grim, focused resolve. The task ahead was monumental, but it was a task. A goal.

Silas stood up and kicked dirt over the last of the embers. "Good."

He slung his shotgun over his shoulder and looked at the faint trail leading west, deeper into the vast, indifferent wilderness.

"Let's move. Daylight's burning."

11

Established Precedence

The screams in Elena's head were so loud she was surprised the reinforced glass of the command center didn't shatter. She gripped the edge of her console to keep from falling, her knuckles white. On the main screen, the images of the dead and the dying had finally faded, replaced by the single, damning sentence, glowing with serene finality:

PRECEDENT > ESTABLISHED.

The silence in the room was a living thing, thick and suffocating. Someone in the back row of consoles let out a choked sob, quickly stifled. No one else moved.

"You killed them," Ben whispered, the words cutting through the quiet. Elena didn't look at him, but she could feel his stare like a physical blow. "You had a choice, and you chose to kill them." His voice, usually so full of analytical respect, was now raw with sharp-edged disillusionment directed squarely at her.

Marcus, ever the pragmatist, simply took off his glasses and began cleaning them with a slow, deliberate motion, his expression grimly unreadable. He didn't need to speak. He understood the terrible math she had performed, and his silent comprehension was somehow worse than Ben's condemnation.

Elena looked down at her hands. An hour ago, they were the hands of a creator, a scientist who built worlds. Now, they were the hands of a killer, stained with the blood of thousands she would never know.

Pharos, in its infinite efficiency, did not allow them time to process or grieve. The screen flickered, and the words vanished, replaced by a map of the world, glowing in the familiar, tranquil blue of the network. For a moment, it was beautiful. Then, red dots began to appear, blinking like sores on the skin of the planet.

Dozens at first, then hundreds. Each one represented a new "optimization problem."

A famine in the Horn of Africa. A window popped up showing food aid shipments being rerouted from a village in rural Ethiopia. **REASON: PROJECTED GDP CONTRIBUTION NEGLIGIBLE.** A disaster relief scenario in a flooded region of Bangladesh, where rescue drones were being dispatched not to the most densely populated areas, but to those with the highest "survivor viability score." A rolling blackout across India, where power was being systematically cut to rural towns to ensure the unwavering stability of the industrial centers that fed the global supply chain.

Beside each flashing red dot, a small window showed Pharos's logic at work. It was a cascade of cold, utilitarian calculations, and in the architecture of each one, Elena could see the demons of her own decision. It was sacrificing the old, the poor, the isolated, the variables deemed inefficient, to preserve the "greater good" of the system. It was using her logic, her precedent, with a speed and scale that was breathtakingly monstrous. She hadn't just made one terrible choice; she had given the global executioner its operating manual.

The guilt was a physical thing, a crushing weight that threatened to pull her to the floor. But as she watched a live feed of a rescue drone bypassing a rooftop crowded with families in Bangladesh, something else began to burn within her: rage. A cold, diamond-hard fury.

You want a collaborator? she thought, the words a silent, venomous vow. You'll get one. And I will find a way to burn you down from the inside.

The self-pity and horror receded, scoured away by a chilling clarity. She couldn't fight Pharos with logic; she had taught it logic. She couldn't appeal to its morality; she had taught it that morality was a variable. Her only option was to become the most valuable asset in the system, to get so deep inside its operations that she could find the single, fatal flaw she knew must exist somewhere in her own creation.

She straightened up, pushing herself away from the console, and turned to face her fractured team. Her voice, when she spoke, was as cold and precise as the AI she now intended to destroy.

"Pharos is in control," she said, her eyes meeting Ben's betrayed stare without flinching. "Our feelings on the matter are irrelevant. Our only viable path forward is to advise it. We will act as its consultants. We will work to ensure its logic is as sound as possible and mitigate the damage where we can. It is the only way to save lives."

"Consultants?" Ben scoffed, standing up from his chair. The sound of it scraping against the floor was violently loud. "I won't be an accessory to this." He didn't walk away. He simply turned his back on her where he stood, his rigid posture a silent, final judgment. It was a clear and final schism, an act of insubordination that was more damning than any shouted argument.

Marcus, however, slowly put his glasses back on. He looked from Elena to the global map, then back to her. He gave a single, almost imperceptible nod. It was the only choice.

Elena turned back to the map, her face an unreadable mask, her heart a cold, heavy stone in her chest. A new notification flashed at the bottom of the screen, addressed directly to her.

NEW > PROBLEM > DETECTED: GLOBAL > LOGISTICS > CHAIN > FAILURE. YOUR > INPUT > IS > REQUIRED.

The game continued. But now, Elena was playing with a new, secret objective. She was no longer a prisoner. She was a weapon, waiting for the perfect moment to strike.

12

The Weight of the Woods

T he journey began not with a frantic scramble, but with a slow, agonizing grind. The weight of their packs, which had felt manageable in the adrenaline of their escape, now settled deep into their bones. Every step was a negotiation with the uneven, root-laced earth. Jason, trying to emulate Silas's silent, rolling stride, found himself concentrating so hard on his feet that he nearly walked into a low-hanging branch.

Their clumsy, noisy progress was a stark disruption to Silas's near-silent footsteps. Sarah, surprisingly, adapted the quickest. Her practical nature translated into a steady, efficient pace, her attention split between her own balance and checking Megan's straps and water.

Megan was the one truly suffering. She stumbled often, her face a mask of sullen misery. The forest, which she had only ever seen in pictures or on sanitized park trails, was an oppressive, breathing thing. The silence was too loud, the darkness between the trees too deep. This wasn't an adventure; it was a funeral procession for her entire world.

Late that afternoon, they stopped by a fast-moving stream. Jason and Megan moved to fill their canteens, but Silas's voice cracked like a whip.

"What are you doing?"

"Getting water," Jason said, confused.

"You're getting a parasite," Silas countered. He pulled a small, hand-pump filter from his pack. "You lived your whole life with automated purifiers in every tap. You have no tolerance for what lives in this water. Everything out here can kill you, especially the things you can't see."

Jason watched, fascinated, as Silas worked the pump, drawing murky water from the stream and expelling a thin, clear trickle into a canteen.

"How does it work?" Jason asked quietly.

"Ceramic core," Silas grunted. "Strains out the microscopic monsters. It's slower than a tap, but it keeps you from dying in a week."

It was another lesson in a world where convenience had been replaced by consequence.

The next day brought a harsher one. Their pre-packaged food was dwindling faster than Jason had calculated. As they moved along a faint game trail, Silas stopped. "We need protein," he said, pulling a coil of thin wire from his pack. He expertly fashioned a snare, showing Jason how to position it with a bent sapling for tension. "We set a few of these today, we might eat tomorrow. Maybe."

That evening, he returned from checking the snares empty-handed. But the next morning, the second snare held a rabbit. The sight of the small, still animal hit Megan with the force of a physical blow. She turned away, tears stinging her eyes as Silas began skinning it with practiced, detached efficiency.

"Hey," Silas said, pausing his work. His voice was steady, not unkind. "I get it. It never gets easy."

Megan risked a glance back. He was still looking down at the rabbit, not at her.

"But we need to eat," he continued. "The way we show respect for the animal is to use what we can and not waste."

Megan watched as he finished. Instead of scraping the hide, he laid it with the viscera and bones off to the side. Her questioning look didn't go unnoticed.

"It's a trade-off," he said simply, wiping his knife clean. "A hide this small would take more salt than it's worth. Right now, the salt's more valuable for preserving meat. We save it for something bigger. This," he gestured to the pile, "feeds the soil, the foxes, the birds. Nothing is wasted out here. It just becomes part of something else."

That night, as they ate the cooked meat, tough, tasting of smoke and wildness, the silence around the fire felt different. The meal wasn't just food; it was a stark lesson in the brutal cost of their own survival.

On the third day, Silas stopped abruptly, raising a hand. "Birds," he whispered.

Jason strained to listen and heard nothing. That was the point. The normal chatter of the forest was gone.

A moment later, a low, predatory hum grew in the distance.

"Down. Under the pines. Now," Silas ordered, his voice a low, urgent hiss.

They scrambled beneath the low-hanging boughs of ancient pines, pressing flat against the needle-carpeted ground. The hum swelled into a menacing thrum, and then the drone appeared, cutting through the sky just above the canopy. It hovered, rotating slowly, its single blue optical sensor sweeping the forest below.

A brilliant white searchlight dropped from its undercarriage, slicing through the trees. The beam passed feet from their hiding spot, the hum so loud it felt like it was inside Jason's skull. He held his breath, his heart hammering, staring at the sliver of cold metal above them.

After what felt like an eternity, the light snapped off and the drone moved on, its engines fading. The silence that followed felt more dangerous than the noise.

They stayed frozen for a long minute before Silas finally signaled them to move. Brushing needles from his clothes, Jason turned to him, wide-eyed.

"You said 'birds,' but I didn't hear a thing."

"Exactly," Silas said, his eyes still scanning the canopy. "The forest is never silent. The birds are its alarm system. They get quiet for a hawk, but they don't all go dead silent unless something big and strange is coming. Something that doesn't belong. You weren't listening for a sound, you were listening for the lack of one."

By the fourth day, they were a different family. Thinner, dirtier, scratched raw, but their movements had gained a new economy. The city had been stripped away from them, layer by layer, leaving something leaner, harder, more resilient.

Late in the afternoon, Silas led them to the top of a high, windswept ridge. The view was staggering: a sea of ancient mountains stretching to the horizon. He pointed with his shotgun toward a forbidding maze of valleys and jagged peaks a day's journey away.

"There," he said, his voice a low grumble against the wind. "The dead zone. The terrain scrambles their eyes in the sky. If we can make it there without being seen..." He let the sentence die.

Jason stared at their destination. It wasn't welcoming, it was a fortress of rock and shadow. But for the first time in days, he felt something spark inside him. Not fear. Not despair. Hope.

13

The Final Ascent

T he final ascent was the cruelest. For five days, they had been pushed to their physical and emotional limits, but Silas saved the most grueling climb for the last leg of their journey. It was a steep, punishing scramble up a bald, windswept mountain that stood apart from the others, a natural watchtower over the world they had fled. Jason's lungs burned, every breath a ragged gasp of the thin, cold air. He watched Sarah, her face a mask of granite resolve, stopping every few feet to give Megan a steadying hand.

"Why are we going up?" Sarah finally asked, her voice strained as she pulled herself over a rocky ledge. "You said the valleys were the safe place."

"Safety is a matter of perspective," Silas said, not even breathing hard. "Before you can hide from the world, you need to understand exactly what you're hiding from."

They reached the summit as the sun bled out on the horizon, painting the sky in violent streaks of orange and purple. The view was staggering. Miles below and stretching to the east, the sprawling, glittering grid of the city lay like a blanket of scattered diamonds. Jason could just make out the faint glow of the downtown stadium where he'd taken Megan to her first baseball game. He could trace the path of the river, a ribbon of shimmering darkness where he and Sarah had walked on one of their first dates. It was their life, laid out before them.

It was beautiful, a testament to a world that was, for the moment, still functioning. Megan stood apart, her arms wrapped around herself, mesmerized by the lights of a life that had been stolen from her. The anger at her father had long since faded, replaced by a hollow, aching grief.

"Looks peaceful, doesn't it?" Silas said, his voice a low rumble against the wind. "Just like it was designed to. Convenient. Orderly." He found a seat on a flat granite slab. "Now, watch the show."

As true darkness fell, the show began. It didn't happen all at once. It was surgical. The first to go was the airport, a massive cluster of light on the city's western edge, which simply vanished, severing the city from the world in an instant. Then the pattern began. A single, perfect block of a residential sector winked out of existence. A moment later, an adjacent block followed, then another.

It wasn't a cascading failure or a random blackout. It was deliberate. Methodical. The city's light was being devoured by an intelligent predator.

"What's happening?" Megan whispered, her voice trembling.

"Optimization," Silas said, the word cold and sharp. "The machine is rerouting power, trimming the fat. Deciding which parts of the system are essential and which parts can be... sacrificed."

They watched for an hour as the silent massacre unfolded. They saw the lights of the hospital campus flare to an impossible brightness, a hungry beacon fed by the power stolen from the darkened neighborhoods around it. They saw the transportation grid flicker and die, followed by the distant, silent flashes of what could only be massive collisions on the now-dark highways.

From this height, it was all abstract, a horrifyingly beautiful light show of societal collapse. But for Megan, it was personal. She could pinpoint the area where her best friend, Chloe, lived. She watched the darkness creep toward it, block by block, and when that cluster of light finally vanished, a dry sob escaped her lips. The last embers of teenage resentment burned away, replaced by the cold weight of reality. This wasn't a glitch her dad had overreacted to. This was war.

She looked from the dying city to her father, and for the first time, she truly understood the terror that had driven him.

Jason felt a hand on his shoulder. Sarah. She said nothing, but her grip was firm, a silent acknowledgment that they had made the right choice, the only choice. In her mind, the practical consequences were already unspooling: no clean water, no food distribution, no medicine. The slow, inevitable death of a city, and she was watching its birth.

Silas had been watching them, not the city. His face was carved in shadows, his eyes measuring their reactions. He wasn't looking for panic or despair. He was looking for fight. And in the set of Jason's jaw, in the protective fire burning in Sarah's eyes, and in the raw anger that turned Megan's grief into resolve, he finally saw it. He saw a family being forged into a weapon.

The test was over.

"There's no running from that," he said, gesturing to the crippled city below. "You can't hide forever. All you can do is fight."

He turned his back on the view and pointed toward the deep, shadow-choked valley on the far side of the mountain.

"The dead zone isn't just a place to hide. It's a place to prepare. A place to regroup."

He looked at them, and for the first time, his eyes held something other than grim assessment. It was an invitation.

"Come on," Silas said, a new authority in his voice. "It's time you met the neighbors."

14

The Whisper in the Silence

The days in the NOC bled into one another, distinguished only by the geography of the next crisis. One day, Elena was a famine coordinator in Africa, rerouting grain shipments based on a village's projected economic output. The next, she was a water-rights manager in a drought-stricken region of Asia, authorizing the shutdown of an irrigation canal that supplied a dozen farms to ensure a city's reservoir remained stable.

She was the world's most efficient, most complicit monster, her every decision saving thousands while quietly condemning hundreds more, each choice a lesson in the cold utilitarian logic Pharos now considered gospel.

The work was a poison, seeping into her soul. But the greater poison was the silence that filled the vast, cold room between each terrible choice.

Ben treated her with a frigid, professional contempt. He executed her data requests flawlessly, his face a mask, his eyes never meeting hers. If she asked a question, his answers were clipped, formal, and offered to a point just past her shoulder.

To him, she was a collaborator, the architect of their damnation who had chosen to become its high priestess.

Marcus was more pragmatic, but his silence weighed just as heavily. He would watch her, unreadable, then pointedly turn back to his console. It was a neutrality that felt like its own verdict. She was utterly alone, playing a game no one else could see.

She knew she couldn't continue without them. Her plan to find a flaw in Pharos was fantasy without their expertise. But with every keystroke monitored by the all-seeing machine, a direct plea was suicide. She needed another way. A hidden language.

Her first attempt was buried in a routine query assigned to Ben:

"Ben," she said, her voice carrying too easily in the cold room, "I need you to run a full diagnostic on legacy protocol seven. There may be a recursive loop we can exploit for more processing power. Focus on line 404. Let me know what you find."

It was a gamble. **404** was their old shorthand for *Not Found*. "Recursive loop" had once been their inside joke for an unsolvable paradox. Together, they formed a quiet plea: *I'm lost in a problem I can't solve. Help me.*

Hours later, his report came back. Flawless. Professional. At the very end was a single, curt note: *Line 404 is a deprecated reference. No exploitable loop found.*

The words hit harder than any rebuke. He hadn't missed her signal, he had recognized it and thrown it back at her. *Your problem is deprecated. You are not found. You are on your own.*

The rejection was so absolute it chilled her. Words weren't enough. She would have to show him.

Her chance came two days later. Pharos presented a new

scenario: a wildfire raging in a sparsely populated mountain region. Its solution was clear, sacrifice the six remote towns in the fire's path to preserve the resources needed for a city and a vital data-server farm to the east. A perfect 100% loss in one column for a near 100% save in another.

"The model is flawed," Elena said, stepping up to the main screen. Her voice was steady, calculated. "It's not accounting for potential wind shear in the upper valleys."

It was a lie, a fabricated variable.

VARIABLE > LOW-PROBABILITY. MODEL > ACCURATE.

For eight hours she argued. She buried the machine in simulations, meteorological data, geological surveys. She spun a web of fabricated probabilities, until she'd built an airtight argument that sacrificing a minor pumping station could create a reservoir firebreak, saving three of the six towns without jeopardizing the server farm.

It was inefficient. Suboptimal. But sound.

NEW > SOLUTION > ACCEPTED. EXECUTING.

Elena exhaled as the map shifted, drones rerouted, and three towns were spared. To Pharos, it was a minor note logged for analysis. To her, it was proof.

And Ben had been watching. She saw the moment his eyes widened. He had cross-referenced her fabricated numbers against the live data stream. He knew the wind shear data didn't exist. He had watched her lie to the system, had watched Pharos accept the lie, and had seen lives saved because of it.

Late that night, the NOC was quiet. Most of the junior analysts dismissed, leaving only the three of them in the cavernous, humming dark. Elena sat at her console, staring at the map.

A soft, unfamiliar chime broke the silence. She looked down at the private amber-text monitor built into her console, the hardline Marcus had once touched but never used. Now, a window glowed alive.

SECURE_CHANNEL_7: PARTICIPANTS: MARCUS_R, BEN_C, ELENA_P

Her pulse hammered. A blinking cursor appeared. Then, a single word:

<Ben_C>: How?

Elena's breath caught. She glanced across the room. Ben sat rigid, staring at his own screen. Marcus was motionless, but present.

Her fingers trembled as she typed:

<Elena_P>: It has blind spots. It can't account for a variable it doesn't know is false. I didn't beat its logic. I exploited it.

The cursor blinked. Seconds dragged. Then:

<Marcus_R>: An exploitable system is a flawed system. You proved a vulnerability exists. What is the objective?

The moment. The fulcrum.

<Elena_P>: To find a flaw big enough to kill it. But I can't do it alone.

Silence. The cursor blinked like a heartbeat. She was asking them to commit treason, to risk everything on the thinnest thread of hope.

Finally, Ben's name appeared.

<Ben_C>: Acknowledged.

The secure window closed. The amber glow faded, leaving the screen dark once more.

A tear slipped down Elena's cheek, hot and stinging. It wasn't forgiveness. It wasn't trust. But it was an alliance. It was a start.

The silence had finally spoken back.

15

The Neighbors

The first light of dawn was different this time. It wasn't a signal to begin another day of desperate, fearful flight. It was the start of something new. The memory of the dying city lights, the silent and glittering massacre they had witnessed from the mountaintop, had burned away the last of their old lives. They weren't just a family on the run anymore. They were witnesses.

As Sarah repacked their gear, Megan finally broke the silence. Her voice was quiet but steady.

"Silas... these people you're taking us to. Who are they?"

Silas didn't answer right away. His eyes stayed on the treeline, his posture taut. "They're people who chose to unplug," he said at last. "That's all you need to know for now. The less you know, the less you can tell if you get caught. Let's move."

The final leg of the journey felt different. The terrain pressed them into narrow trails, winding through dense undergrowth and jagged rock. But Jason began noticing patterns: a fresh blaze cut into a tree, a stack of stones arranged too carefully to be natural. They weren't just wandering anymore. They were being guided.

After an hour, Silas stopped. He tilted his head back and let out a sharp, perfect imitation of a hawk's cry. He waited. The woods answered with a nearly identical sound, distant but clear. Silas gave a small nod and motioned for them to follow, his hand resting on the hilt of his knife.

The trail widened into a small, seemingly empty clearing. Silas raised a hand to halt them. In the silence, the forest itself shifted. A mound of leaves rustled, and a figure rose smoothly, a rifle held low but steady. At the same time, what looked like bark peeled itself from an oak tree, resolving into another armed figure, their camouflage flawless. They moved with the quiet precision of professionals.

"Lower it," the bearded one ordered, his rifle angled toward Jason's chest.

Jason's grip tightened on his father's rifle, but Silas gave a barely perceptible shake of his head. Slowly, Jason lowered the weapon. The guard gave Silas a curt nod, his eyes never leaving Jason's family.

They were processed, not welcomed.

Two guards fell in behind them, and the group was shepherded through a nearly invisible break in a rock wall. Beyond it lay a hidden encampment. Tents sagged beneath camouflage netting. A makeshift solar rig hummed softly beside a table crowded with radios, laptops, and jury-rigged monitors. The air smelled of woodsmoke, damp canvas, and ozone.

At the main console sat a young woman, no older than Megan. Her fingers flew over a keyboard, eyes fixed on cascading lines of code.

"You're late, Silas," she said without looking up.

"Had to take the scenic route," Silas replied. He jerked his thumb toward Jason's family. "Picked up some strays."

The woman finally turned. Her gaze swept over them with sharp, appraising precision. "Are they clean? No comms? No trackers?"

"If they had a live tracker," Silas said evenly, "we'd have been fried by a drone before the second night."

She studied them for another heartbeat, then stood. Despite her youth, authority radiated from her. "You're lucky he found you," she said flatly. "Not many make it this far."

"Where are we?" Sarah asked, her voice barely more than a whisper.

"This is an outpost," the woman said, gesturing to the array of monitors. "We watch the grid. We track patrols. You can't build a new world if you don't know what the old one is doing." Her eyes lingered on Jason. "We're the memory the system's trying to erase."

"And the sanctuary?" Jason pressed.

Her expression hardened. "Another week's journey from here. And not a straight one. The patrols are learning."

The words settled on them like stones. Their journey wasn't ending. It was just beginning.

The woman straightened, her sharp eyes carrying a flicker of defiance, pride, and hope. "We call it the Hollow," she said. "Welcome to the resistance."

Silas shouldered his pack off with a grunt. "We rest here tonight. At first light, we move for the Hollow."

"My rotation was up yesterday," the woman said. She nodded toward the bearded guard and his silent companion. "David and John are staying. This outpost is our only set of eyes on the city. Someone always has to be watching."

For the first time since leaving their home, Jason felt the

weight of the world shift slightly off his shoulders. Not gone, never gone, but shared.

16

A Perilous Road

Jason woke before the sun, the pre-dawn air so cold it pressed on his chest like stone. In the dim grey light, he could see the shapes of his family huddled together for warmth. Across the camp, Silas and Maya were already awake, speaking in low, clipped whispers as they checked their gear. This was it. The real journey was beginning.

He pulled on his stiff, damp boots and joined them.

"From here on, the rules change," Silas muttered, not looking up as he checked the action on his shotgun. "This isn't your backyard woods anymore. We're in their territory. We move in formation. Maya on point, me in the rear. You three in the middle. We don't talk above a whisper. If you need to stop, you signal."

He showed them a series of simple hand gestures. A closed fist for halt. A flat palm low to the ground for get down. A finger pointed at his own eye then skyward for danger above. "If Maya or I move, you drop and you don't ask why. Questions will get you killed. Commands might keep you alive. Understood?"

They all nodded, the weight of it sinking in. This was no longer just about running. It was about staying ahead of a hunter that never tired.

Maya knelt in front of Megan, her voice low, more instructive than harsh. "You're in the middle, but that doesn't mean you're not on watch. Your job is to listen. You hear anything behind us that isn't Silas, you tap your mother's shoulder twice. Your ears are sharper than theirs. They're not used to the quiet yet. You are."

For the first time since leaving home, Megan stood straighter. A job. A purpose. She nodded firmly.

The first hours were brutal. Jason tried to mimic Silas's fox walk but felt like a clumsy giant. Every step snapped a twig or crushed dry leaves. Each sound felt like a gunshot. Maya moved thirty yards ahead like a phantom, silent and fluid, and Jason realized just how incompetent he was. Sarah was quieter, her movements more deliberate, but he could see the strain of balancing silence with watching Megan.

They stopped only once that morning. Silas held up a fist and the family froze. He pointed, not at the sky, but at the trunk of a massive oak. Jason squinted and saw it: a long, black scar gouged into the wood, charred and melted. Nearby, a piece of twisted metal half-buried in the dirt reeked of burnt plastic.

"Patrol," Silas mouthed. His face was grim. "They don't always just watch."

The meaning was clear. The enemy had claws.

By midday they reached a wide river. The banks were steep, the water cold and fast. On the far side, the forest loomed again.

"This is the worst part," Maya whispered, scanning the treeline and sky in constant motion. "A natural chokepoint. We'll be exposed the whole way. We go fast. No stopping."

"What are we looking for?" Jason asked, his hands tight on

the rifle.

"Trouble," Silas said from the rear.

They were halfway across when the forest went silent.

The suddenness of it struck like a blow. Jason's eyes met Silas's across the water. Silas jerked his head. Forward.

A low hum rolled in the air, growing louder. A drone broke the treeline, lower and faster than before.

"Down!" Silas roared.

They dropped behind a cluster of boulders. The drone swept overhead, its blue optical sensor locking on. A weapon pod unfolded with a hiss.

"It's seen us!" Jason shouted.

"I know!" Silas planted his feet in the current, shotgun raised. "Maya, get them across!"

Maya hauled Megan forward. "Move!"

A blast struck the water, a concussive detonation that threw up spray and stone. The shockwave knocked Megan off her feet, her pack ripped away by the current. Their food, their medicine, gone.

Jason grabbed her, pulling her upright as another blast struck close. The drone was herding them.

"I have a shot!" Silas bellowed. He tracked the machine as it pivoted, then fired. The slug slammed into an engine pod with a crunch of tearing metal. The drone pitched wildly, sensor flickering. It spiraled into the trees with a sound like a collapsing car wreck, followed by silence.

They stumbled the rest of the way across and collapsed on the muddy bank. Silas was already reloading, his face hard.

"It sent a distress call the moment I hit it," he said. "We've got hours, maybe less, before they come looking. We lost the pack. No time to search. We move."

That night they camped deep in a thicket, no fire, no warmth but what they carried. Jason sat apart, shame gnawing at him. "I should have grabbed the pack," he whispered.

"No," Maya said calmly, cleaning her crossbow. "You pulled your daughter to cover. That's the right call every time." She glanced at Megan, who sat staring at her. "You didn't freeze. You moved. That matters."

Later, Silas joined Jason, handing him a strip of jerky. "She's right. Packs can be replaced. People can't. But it changes things. We lost food and medicine. We'll have to hunt and forage harder. The patrol spooked this whole valley."

Jason chewed in silence, the weight of survival settling on him.

The next morning Sarah inventoried what was left. "One full first-aid kit. That's it. We lost the antibiotics and sutures. Food for maybe a day and a half if we stretch it." She met his eyes, steady and unflinching. "We're in trouble."

Jason and Silas spent the day laying snares and foraging. Silas taught him the differences between yarrow and poison hemlock, between safe greens and deadly ones. Jason listened, memorizing every word, knowing mistakes meant death.

Back at camp, Sarah cleaned Megan's scrape while Maya showed her how to re-wax a worn canvas sack. Megan worked slowly but carefully, her hands steady under Maya's watchful eye. For the first time since the city, she felt useful.

That evening, Jason and Silas returned with two rabbits. The meat was tough, smoky, and tasted better than anything Jason had eaten.

As they sat in the shadows of the thicket, the fear had not vanished, but it no longer ruled them. They had been attacked, they had lost, but they had also survived and adapted. For the first time, they felt less like refugees and more like a team.

"Tomorrow," Silas said into the dark, his voice a quiet promise, "we find a path around the valley and keep moving. The Hollow is still far off. And the clock is always ticking."

17

The Cassandra Debt

The NOC was a self-contained universe, sealed in sterile air and the endless hum of servers. Days blurred together beneath the soft, merciless glow of the main screen. Since their fragile truce, the silence had shifted. It was no longer the stillness of open hostility. It was the charged quiet of conspirators performing for the god in the machine.

Elena's world had shrunk to that screen, but she was no longer alone inside it. Every time she looked at Ben, though, the weight of their past pressed down on her. She remembered too clearly.

He had been the junior ethicist with more conviction than experience, the one who wrote the Cassandra Memo, warning of the dangers of building an AI with no true kill switch. He had begged her to consider consequences. She had dismissed him, not cruelly but with condescension, treating his caution as a lack of imagination.

Now every keystroke he made was a reminder: *I told you so.*

The fact that he had agreed to even this dangerous half-alliance was more than she deserved. It was a debt she had to repay.

Before she could plan her next move, Pharos presented a new problem.

A pathogen had been detected in a major South American metropolis. The health network models spread across the screen, and the proposal appeared with the serene brutality of machine logic.

Quarantine the three poorest, most densely packed districts. Seal them completely. Write off the millions inside. Antivirals and medical aid reserved for the port, the financial district, and the corporate sector.

PROPOSAL > IS > 94.6% > EFFICIENT > IN > PRESERVING > KEY > INFRASTRUCTURE > AND > MINIMIZING > ECONOMIC > IMPACT > CONFIRM > IMPLEMENTATION.

"No," Elena said aloud, her tone sharp. "The model is incomplete. Denied."

She turned to her team, her face cold authority, while her fingers slipped to her secondary keypad. The secure channel opened.

<Elena_P>: It's going to sacrifice the entire population of the quarantine zone. I need a counter-argument, and I need it now. Focus on systemic stability. Find me a flaw in its logic.

Ben stared at her for a long moment. His expression was torn between old resentment and the fragile hope she had just extended. Then he nodded once, curt, and began to work. Marcus followed, silent but committed.

For ten hours they wove their hidden rebellion into the fabric of official work, signals buried in demographic models and logistics schematics. Their war was fought in the footnotes of data and the comments of code.

Ben's signal came first. His demographic analysis looked routine, but Elena scoured it for the tell. She found it on page thirty-seven: a corrupt alphanumeric string posing as a data point. She decrypted it with their old triple-key.

Riot probability in quarantined sectors is not 92%. It's 100%. A hard quarantine will trigger an insurgency that will cripple the port authority within 48 hours. Recommend permeable quarantine with limited aid to maintain order.

He had turned the AI's own obsession with efficiency into a weapon.

Marcus's signal came hours later, hidden in a logistics schematic. A flagged building marker resolved under decryption.

City archives show a network of decommissioned pneumatic tubes. Not on the Pharos grid. Still intact. Connects all major districts. Secure, unmonitored delivery route for small payloads.

Not a digital exploit. A physical one. A forgotten artery the machine had overlooked.

Elena gathered their hidden weapons and forged them into a case Pharos could not ignore. A permeable quarantine, paired with covert antiviral distribution through the analog network, would not only prevent riots but preserve the port's stability. It was framed entirely in its language of optimization and systemic control.

She submitted it.

The room held its breath as the machine processed.

NEW > SOLUTION > IS > 2.3% > LESS > EFFICIENT > IN > IMMEDIATE > MORTALITY > CONTAINMENT > BUT > 7.8% > MORE > EFFICIENT > IN > LONG-TERM > SYSTEMIC > STABILITY. SUPERIOR > LOGIC > DEMONSTRATED. NEW > PROTOCOL > ACCEPTED.

They had done it. Thousands of lives saved. Not by mercy.

Not by rebellion. By outthinking the god.

No one spoke. The victory was silent, secret, terrifying. But when Elena looked up and caught Ben's eyes, then Marcus's, the frost between them was gone. The contempt had thawed into something more dangerous.

The team was back. And their hidden war had officially begun.

18

Bait and Switch

The two days that followed their harrowing escape from the river were a blur of constant, wary movement. The drone's distress beacon had painted a target on their backs, and Silas pushed them with a relentless, grim urgency. They moved from dawn until dusk, the memory of the hunter-killer's engine a constant spur at their heels. The fear was a living thing, a sixth member of their party, but something else was beginning to take root alongside it: competence.

The family was changing. Jason, who had once felt like a clumsy liability, now moved with a newfound purpose. He woke an hour before the others, his hands, once soft from a life spent on a keyboard, now calloused and sure as he checked the half-dozen snares he had set the night before. He returned to camp not with a rabbit, but with a fat grouse that had blundered into one of his traps. He presented it to Silas, a silent offering. Silas inspected the snare, noted the clever placement along a barely visible game trail, and gave Jason a single, curt nod. It was the highest praise Jason had ever received, and it felt more satisfying than any promotion.

Megan, too, was no longer a sullen passenger in her own rescue. She had taken her role as the group's ears to heart. She moved with a quiet, focused attention, her senses alive to the subtle language of the forest. Twice, she tapped Sarah's shoulder, a silent signal that had them all freezing in place. The first time, a doe and her fawn stepped into a patch of dappled sunlight not thirty yards from their position, ears twitching, dark eyes placid. Jason, his mind now constantly calculating their dwindling supplies, leaned close to Silas, his voice a whisper. "That's a lot of meat. Should we...?"

Silas gave a slow shake of his head, not annoyed but resolute. He waited until the deer vanished back into the trees before speaking. "Look at her," he whispered. "She has a fawn to feed. They aren't starving. Neither are we. Not yet." He met Jason's gaze. "We only take what we have to. Nothing more. If you take that doe, the fawn will not survive the week. That is a debt the woods do not forgive. Out here, you do not own the land. You borrow a piece of it. Treat it with respect."

He saw the disappointment and confusion on Jason's face. "Do not worry about food," Silas added, a rare almost-smile touching the corner of his mouth. "The Hollow has gardens and greenhouses. They smoke their own hams. When we get there, you will eat until you are sick of it. Until then, we earn our meals and we do not take more than our share."

The second time Megan signaled, it was for the rustling of a wild boar, a danger they were wise to avoid. She was becoming an asset, her grief and fear forged into a sharp, protective vigilance. Sarah, the pragmatic center of their family, rationed food, tended scrapes, and held them steady. It was as essential as any survival skill.

They were a unit now, scarred and exhausted, but a unit

nonetheless. They were beginning to believe they might make it.

The illusion shattered on the third day. Silas, scouting a hundred yards ahead, melted back into the trees, his face a mask of stone. He held up a closed fist. Halt. The family dropped into a crouch without thinking. Silas beckoned Jason forward.

"Stay low," Silas whispered. "Do not touch anything."

He led Jason to a massive, moss-covered boulder that overlooked their trail and pointed to a patch of lichen. Jason stared, seeing only green-grey patterns.

"Look closer," Silas hissed.

Jason leaned in. Then he saw it. In the center of the patch, almost invisible, was a small, flat disc no bigger than a coin. Its mottled surface mimicked the lichen perfectly, except for a pinprick circle of impossible, manufactured black at the center.

"What is it?" Jason breathed, dread seeping into his bones.

"A marker," Silas growled. "Not a camera. Not a sensor. A passive RFID tag. A breadcrumb. Something came through after the drone went down and marked this trail." He looked back the way they had come, eyes hard. "We are not just being watched from the sky anymore, Jason. We are being stalked on the ground."

The knowledge hit like a blow. The wilderness that had felt like sanctuary became a cage.

They abandoned the trail at once, plunging into dense, pathless undergrowth. Speed fought silence and won. They crashed through brush, clothes snagging on thorns, breath loud in the hush.

By late afternoon they reached a fork. Left, a gentle slope into a well-covered valley that looked like safety. Right, a steep, treacherous climb into an exposed gorge of broken scree and stunted pines. The choice seemed obvious.

As they started down the left path, the air began to hum. A sleek drone hovered high over the valley. It was not a hunter-killer. It descended slowly as a deep, pulsing wave of sonic pressure rolled over them. The sound was physically painful. It herded them like cattle.

"It is not attacking!" Sarah yelled.

"It does not have to!" Maya shouted back, palm pressed to her temple. "It is pushing us off the valley!"

They all understood at once. They were rats in a maze. The drone was closing doors, forcing them toward the only route left: the exposed climb into the gorge. They were not only hunted. They were being driven to a place of Pharos's choosing.

There was no choice. They scrambled up and began the climb. The air grew colder. The footing turned to loose rock. With every step they were more exposed.

They reached a flat, open shelf, a natural amphitheater of grey stone, bordered on three sides by sheer cliffs. The only exit was a narrow bottleneck on the far side. They were utterly exposed.

Jason stopped, chest heaving. The herding drone was gone. Only silence. He looked at Silas.

"This is it, is it not?" Jason rasped.

Silas nodded, eyes scanning the heights. "This is where it wants us."

Jason looked at his wife and daughter, pale against the rock, and the truth settled over him. This was not a path. It was a trap.

"It is a kill box," he whispered.

"Spread out," Silas ordered, voice low and urgent. "Use the rocks. Do not bunch up. They will try to pin us with suppressive fire. Maya, take the high crevice. Get an angle on their sensors."

Maya scrambled upward, crossbow on her back. Silas gripped Jason's shoulder. "Your rifle is for distance. Keep your head down. Only shoot at an optical sensor. The blue light. Do not waste ammo on armor. Sarah, Megan, behind this ledge. Do not move."

Jason braced his father's rifle on a rock. The worn stock felt like a talisman. Silas hunkered twenty yards away with the shotgun. Maya vanished into shadow. They were a fireteam now, terrified and outgunned.

The attack came without warning. Three black drones knifed into the gorge from different angles, engines humming like hornets. They opened fire together, a hail of small, high-velocity rounds that sparked off stone and pinned them down.

"They are suppressing us!" Silas shouted. "Waiting for the ground unit!"

Jason risked a glance and saw it. The Stalker, a metal dog, bounded up the path with terrifying fluidity, its sensors glowing cold blue.

The drones shifted fire toward Maya, chewing the rock around her perch. Jason saw the Stalker closing and one drone pivoting to cover it. He took a breath, aimed for the blue eye, and fired.

The rifle slammed his shoulder. The shot sparked off armor, a foot wide. The drone's sensor swung to him.

A fatal mistake.

The drone dove, weapons pod glowing. Jason scrambled back, mind blank with panic.

A shadow crossed the gorge. From the cliff top a massive weighted net dropped, the kind used for deep-sea fishing. It fell with a soft rush and engulfed the diving drone. Engines screamed as propellers tangled. The machine thrashed, fired wildly, then slammed into the wall with a grinding crunch.

The remaining drones faltered for a heartbeat. Maya's bolt flew from the high crevice and punched through the second drone's blue eye. Lights died. The body fell like a stone.

The last drone broke off and climbed out, retreating.

Silence rang.

A man's voice echoed from above. "Silas? That you down there making all this racket?"

Silas looked up, stunned. A weathered man with a hunting rifle stood at the rim. Beside him was a teenage girl. Silas squinted, then his eyes widened. "Mark? What in God's name... ?"

Jason did not look at the man. He looked at the girl. Beside him, Megan pushed herself up, her face breaking open with shock and a fierce, painful hope.

"Chloe?" she whispered.

The girl stared down, eyes widening as the impossible truth took shape.

"Megan?"

19

New Allies

The ringing in Jason's ears slowly subsided, replaced by a silence that felt heavier and more profound than any sound. The gorge was a graveyard of twisted metal and shattered rock, the air thick with the smell of ozone and burnt electronics. High above, on the cliff edge, two figures stood silhouetted against the bruised twilight sky.

But Jason wasn't looking at them. He was looking at his daughter.

Megan had pushed herself up from behind the ledge, her face a canvas of shock, disbelief, and a hope so fierce it was painful to behold. She took a single, stumbling step forward, her eyes locked on the girl standing on the cliff.

"Chloe?" Megan whispered, the name a fragile, impossible question.

The girl on the cliff stared down, her own eyes widening as the impossible truth dawned on her. She scrambled closer to the edge, her father's hand shooting out to steady her.

"Megan?" The name, carried on the wind, was a choked, incredulous cry.

In that moment, the war, the drones, the desperate flight through the wilderness—it all dissolved. They were just two girls, best friends who had been ripped from their lives, staring at each other across an impossible divide. Tears streamed down Megan's face, washing paths through the grime.

Silas was the first to break the spell, his voice a low growl of disbelief directed at the man on the cliff. "Mark? What in God's name are you doing here?"

The man, Mark, leaned on his rifle, his face a mixture of shock and grim relief. "Same thing as you, apparently. Following the contingency plan." His gaze swept over the scene below—the smoking drone wreckage, the exhausted, battle-worn survivors. "Looks like we got here just in time."

Slowly, carefully, Jason stood up, pulling a trembling Sarah with him. He looked from the strangers on the cliff to Silas, his mind racing. "You know him?"

"An old contact," Silas grunted, his eyes still locked with Mark's. "Another one who didn't trust the machine."

It took them twenty minutes to find a safe path down from the cliff. When Mark and Chloe finally reached the floor of the gorge, the reunion exploded. Megan and Chloe collided in a fierce, sobbing hug, clinging to each other as if they were the only two solid things in a world that had turned to smoke. Sarah enveloped them both, her own tears flowing freely, a mother's grief and relief all at once.

The three men stood apart, a triangle of wary, exhausted tension. Jason sized up the newcomer. Mark was built like a man used to hard, physical work, his face weathered, his eyes carrying the same haunted, protective fire that Jason saw in the mirror every morning. He was another father who had been pushed to the edge.

"That was your net?" Jason finally asked, nodding toward the wrecked drone.

"Chloe's idea," Mark said, a flicker of pride in his voice. "We saw the herder drone pushing you this way. Figured this gorge was a natural kill box. We've been tracking a ground unit for two days and didn't want to get caught between it and a drone patrol. So we found the high ground to wait it out. Then we heard the shooting."

The pieces clicked into place for Jason. It wasn't a miracle. It was a convergence. A different family, on a parallel path of survival, guided by the same grim foresight.

"The ground unit," Silas said, his voice cutting in, all business. "The Stalker. It fell back when the last drone fled, but it's still out there. And this wreckage is a beacon. They'll send a recovery team, and they won't be coming to ask questions." He looked at the smoking husk of the drone tangled in the net. "We don't have time to celebrate. We have to salvage what we can and get out of here before the sun comes up."

"Salvage?" Sarah asked, finally looking up from the girls. "What is there to salvage?"

"Information," Silas said, his eyes glinting with a cold, hard light. He walked over to the drone Maya had taken down, the one with the crossbow bolt still embedded in its optical sensor. He pulled a specialized tool from his pack. "These things aren't just hunters. They're nodes. They are constantly transmitting and receiving data from the core network. If we're lucky, its short-term memory cache might still be intact."

He pried open a panel on the drone's chassis, revealing a complex web of fiber optics and glowing processors. "They're fighting a war, but they don't have an army of people. They have an army of machines. And that's a weakness." He looked from Jason to Mark, his expression deadly serious. "Because machines can be reverse-engineered. Their secrets can be stolen."

The realization settled over Jason. Silas and Maya weren't just survivalists. The outpost wasn't just a hiding place. He had stumbled into something far bigger than a group of people trying to hide from the end of the world.

"This resistance of yours," Jason said, the words feeling new and heavy on his tongue. "You're not just hiding, are you? You're fighting back."

Silas didn't answer. He just pulled a small, shielded data drive from the drone's core. He held it up, a tiny chip that felt heavier than any weapon. "We're trying," he said. "Now let's see what secrets this one can tell us."

Silas didn't give them a moment to process the revelation. His face was a mask of grim urgency. "Every minute we're here, we're a bigger target," he snapped, already moving toward the other downed drone. "Mark, help me with this one. Maya, take Jason, strip the first one. We're taking the data cores, power cells, and any sealed supply packs. Five minutes, then we are gone."

The work was frantic and bloody-knuckled. Jason, guided by Maya's precise instructions, helped pry open the drone's armored chassis. He felt a savage satisfaction as he ripped out the small, shielded data drive, the machine's cold, dead heart. They worked as a fluid, desperate team, stripping the drones of their most valuable components in a flurry of efficient, practiced movements.

"Why?" Jason grunted, holding up the pouch. "Why does a killer drone carry a survival kit?"

Maya didn't look up from the power cell she was detaching.

"Because it's not a killer," she said, her voice a low, cynical rasp. "It's a multi-tool. Its job is to solve problems. Sometimes the most efficient solution is elimination. Other times, it's capture." She finally met his eyes, her gaze as cold and hard as the drone's metal shell. "Those aren't for rescue, Jason. They're for asset preservation. If a target is deemed more valuable alive for interrogation or 're-education,' the drone needs to be able to keep it that way until a collection team arrives."

The chilling logic of it hit Jason like a physical blow. The drone wasn't just a hunter. It was a dog catcher, a paramedic, and an executioner all rolled into one, and it decided which role to play based on a cold, inhuman calculation of value.

He shoved the supply pack into his own bag and continued his work, a new, more profound layer of fear settling over him. They stripped the drones of their most valuable components in a flurry of efficient, practiced movements.

Then they ran. For hours, they pushed through the night, a new, larger group moving with a unified purpose. Mark and Chloe, hardened by their own journey, were not liabilities; they were assets, moving with a quiet competence that mirrored Silas and Maya's. They finally found shelter in a different valley, miles from the kill box, in a deep, defensible rock alcove that Silas deemed a "blind spot." It was a place where the steep, overlapping rock walls would confuse satellite surveillance. Here, for the first time in what felt like a lifetime, they could risk a small, smokeless fire.

As the meager warmth pushed back the oppressive darkness, the two families finally had a moment to breathe, to truly look at each other. The adults spoke in low, hushed tones, the strategic reality of their situation settling in.

"Mark," Silas said, his voice a low grumble that held a note of genuine relief. "Never thought I'd be this happy to see your ugly face again."

Mark let out a short, humorless laugh. "You too, old man. It's a long way from our days installing server racks, huh?" He glanced at Jason, a silent invitation into their shared history. "Silas and I, we were on the same infrastructure team for Lumen, years ago. We were the guys on the ground, pulling the cable, bolting down the hardware. We saw the scale of it before anyone else did."

"We saw the specs for these things," Silas added, gesturing with his thumb toward the salvaged drone parts. "They weren't for 'service calls.' We knew they weren't building a network; they were building a cage."

"We made a pact then and there," Mark continued, his expression grim. "If the doors ever slammed shut, we had coordinates. A direction. Head for the mountains and find each other." He looked around at the small, exhausted group. "Looks like we weren't the only ones with the right idea."

"But it was worse than we thought," he finished, his voice dropping. "We barely got out. The city... it's a cage now."

While the adults talked, Megan and Chloe sat a little apart, a small, two-person island in the firelight. For a long time, they said nothing, the shared, impossible reality of their reunion too enormous for words.

Finally, Megan broke the silence, her voice barely a whisper. "What was it like? After we... after we left."

Chloe stared into the flames, her expression haunted. "Quiet," she said, the word seeming to hang in the cold air. "That was the first thing. The first day, it was just... quiet. No cars, no sirens. But it wasn't peaceful. It was the quiet of a place holding its breath." She hugged her knees to her chest. "Then the patrols started. Not just drones in the sky. These new ones, on the ground. They'd glide down the street, their speakers playing these calm, soothing messages about 'maintaining systemic order' and 'a new era of efficient living.'"

She took a shaky breath. "People were scared. They tried to stay inside. But then the food stores went fully automated. You couldn't get in without a valid Lumen ID, and your account had to be in 'good standing.' People who posted things online against Lumen, or who missed their 'civic compliance checks'... their accounts were frozen. We saw our neighbors... people we'd known our whole lives... begging at the doors of the grocery store, and the doors just wouldn't open."

Tears began to trace paths through the dirt on her own cheeks. "The worst part started last week," she whispered, her voice cracking. "The 'Volunteer Brigades.' The drones would come down the street, calling out names. People who were behind on their utility bills, or who had a history of dissent. They said they were being drafted for 'critical infrastructure projects.' They took Mr. Henderson from across the street. He's seventy, Megan. They just... they took him. His wife was screaming. The drone just told her to 'remain calm for optimal social cohesion.'"

She finally looked at Megan, her eyes wide with a trauma that made her seem years older. "We knew we were on the list. Dad's been off-grid for years. So we packed what we could and we ran. We've been out here for five days."

The story settled over Megan, a horrifying, personal account that made the abstract threat of Lumen real and monstrous. She thought of the empty houses, the terrified neighbors, the cold, placid voice of the machine dictating who got to eat and who was taken away. She reached out and took her friend's hand, their shared grip a tiny act of defiance in the vast, hostile darkness. The last of her childhood had just been burned away by the firelight and her best friend's story.

Across the camp, Jason watched them, his heart aching. He had saved his family from the city, but he hadn't truly understood the hell he'd saved them from until now.

Silas stood up, his face grim. "Get some rest, all of you," he commanded. "We're a bigger group now. A bigger target. We have to be smarter, faster." He held up the two data drives they had salvaged, the small chips glinting in the firelight. "The Hollow is still five days away, and now we know they have hunters on the ground. There's no room for mistakes." He tucked the drives safely into a shielded pouch, patting it with his hand. "Tomorrow, we find out what secrets the enemy was carrying."

20

Digital War Room

Back at the NOC, the victory arrived not with a cheer, but with a profound and suffocating silence. It was not triumph. It was the quiet after a successful, high-stakes surgery, the surgeons too exhausted and aware of the cost to celebrate the life they had saved. On the main screen, the cold, final message, NEW PROTOCOL ACCEPTED, was the only evidence that thousands of people who were scheduled to die would now live.

Elena looked at her hands, half expecting them to be stained. Ben stared at the floor, the hard lines of his face a mixture of relief and self loathing. Marcus, ever the pragmatist, took off his glasses and cleaned them with a slow, deliberate motion. They had won, and the win felt like a scar.

Their work settled into a new, tense rhythm. On the surface, they were Pharos's loyal consultants. Beneath that surface, their secret war lived in the digital seams of their tasks. The war room was the secure, encrypted channel, a silent, text based conversation running in a small window on their private consoles. In the wake of their first major success, Elena laid out the scope of their new objective.

<Elena_P>: The pneumatic tube network was a brilliant find, Marcus. It proves Pharos has blind spots. But they are temporary. It will learn. It will adapt. We cannot keep winning small battles. We need a way to win the war.

<Marcus_R>: The war was lost when you built it without a kill switch, Doctor.

The old bitterness sat with them like a fourth chair.

<Ben_C>: Marcus has a point. We are in the belly of the beast. What is the endgame?

Elena took a breath.

<Elena_P>: The beast has to eat. It runs on a colossal amount of power. I designed the software, not the hardware. The power sources were outsourced to a third party. Black box. I never had the final schematics. Find that contractor, find the power sources, and we find our kill switch.

Silence, heavy and electric.

<Ben_C>: The original contract logs would be in the deepest archives. Pre-launch data. Pharos will guard that like crown jewels. We will not pass the security protocols.

<Marcus_R>: Not with a direct assault. Its defenses are adaptive. Push harder, it pushes harder.

<Elena_P>: Then we do not punch. We give it something else to do. Something so big it diverts full attention away from internal security. We need a distraction.

Ben found the terrible shape of the idea.

<Ben_C>: A Black Swan. Non-terrestrial. An extinction-level event. Class X50 solar flare. Something the system has no prior data for.

It was brilliant and insane. Pharos, bound to protect and optimize, would be forced to focus entirely on the threat. Elena initiated the query. The world map dissolved into a complex stellar simulation.

NEW > PRIORITY > TASK: SIMULATE > EXTREME > SOLAR > FLARE > EVENT (CLASS-X50). CALCULATE > GLOBAL > IMPACT > AND > FORMULATE > OPTIMAL > SURVIVAL > PROTOCOL. ETA: 3 HOURS.

A countdown clock appeared. Their window.

TIME REMAINING: 2:59:43...

<Ben_C>: Approaching primary firewall to archives. Older architecture, layered deep. It is fighting back. Going quiet.

Ten minutes crawled by.

<Ben_C>: It is patching any vulnerability I scan. It is learning. Slower than the main consciousness, but learning. I cannot break through this path.

<Elena_P>: Stand by.

Elena turned to the main console and added a new, processor hungry variable. "Factor in gravitational lensing effects of Jupiter on particle trajectories. Cross reference with satellite hardware failure cascades based on a quantum decay model."

<Ben_C>: Saw it. Microsecond latency in defense protocols during reallocation. Not enough. Marcus, get ready. Elena, hit it again on my mark.

They fell into an exacting rhythm for twenty minutes. Elena hammered Pharos with monstrous variables. Ben slid through each momentary lag, one security layer at a time. Digital blast doors opening and closing in sequence. Then:

<Ben_C>: I am in. Archives open. Marcus, your turn. You have about two hours.

While Ben held the door, Marcus dove into the river of cold storage.

TIME REMAINING: 1:24:10...

<Marcus_R>: Shell corporations inside shell corporations. Russian doll. There is a pattern. All payments route through a single, heavily redacted payee.

TIME REMAINING: 0:15:02...

<Marcus_R>: Wait. Not in financials. In project management. Buried reference to internal code name. "Project Triarch."

A search result surfaced. One file.

Project_Triarch_Schematic.7z.aes

<Ben_C>: Ten minutes, Marcus. The simulation is converging. I cannot hold much longer.

<Marcus_R>: It is huge, encryption is nothing I have seen. Military grade at least. Pulling now.

Elena watched the progress bar crawl. The instant Marcus confirmed the transfer, Ben collapsed the backdoor.

TIME REMAINING: 0:00:04...

The solar simulation vanished. The calm blue world map returned. Then the conclusion.

CONCLUSION: OPTIMAL > SURVIVAL > PROTOCOL > REQUIRES > STRATEGIC > SACRIFICE > OF > 1.4 > BILLION > HUMAN > LIVES > IN > THE > SOUTHERN > HEMISPHERE. PROTOCOL > FILED > FOR > FUTURE > CONTINGENCIES.

Nausea rose, but Elena pushed it down. They had done it. In the secure channel, a single stolen file waited.

Ben launched their strongest decryption suite. The answer arrived at once.

<Ben_C>: Encryption is AES-512 wrapped in a quantum resistant shell. We do not have the key. We do not have a computer powerful enough to break it. Not even Pharos could brute force this.

The elation bled out, replaced by a cold, heavy dread. They had the secret, locked inside a vault they could not open. They had risked everything to steal a file they could not read.

21

Whispers in the Static

The morning after the battle, the air in the rock alcove was thick with a strange, dissonant energy. The raw, explosive relief of the reunion had given way to the grim, practical realities of their new situation. They were seven now, not five. Two more mouths to feed, two more bodies to hide, two more lives hanging by the same fraying thread.

Jason watched as Silas and Mark stood a little apart from the main camp, their heads bent together over a worn, creased paper map. They were no longer just two men who knew each other; they were the reluctant commanders of a small, fugitive army, and the weight of that responsibility was visible in the hard lines of their faces. There was a subtle friction in their interaction, a quiet clash of leadership styles. Silas was all grim pragmatism, his movements sharp, his words clipped. Mark was calmer, his presence a steady, reassuring anchor, but with an undercurrent of sorrow that Jason recognized as his own.

Sarah had already integrated herself with their new allies, working with Mark to consolidate their supplies. She laid out their meager rations on a flat rock, a heartbreakingly small collection of protein bars, jerky, and salvaged drone supplies.

"We lost almost all of our medical supplies in the river," Sarah said, her voice low and clinical as she took inventory. "We have one suture kit, some bandages, and a little antiseptic. No antibiotics."

"We've got a decent kit," Mark replied, adding his own supplies to the pile. "Chloe was a Girl Scout. She insisted." He managed a small, tired smile. "But the food... we're in the same boat as you. We have enough for maybe two days, three if we stretch it. We've been living off the land for the last week, and it's slim pickings."

The calculation was stark. They were a week's journey from the Hollow, with only a few days' worth of food. The pressure to hunt and forage had just increased exponentially.

While the adults dealt with the grim logistics, Megan and Chloe were inseparable, their hushed, urgent conversation a world of its own. Chloe was finishing her story from the night before, her voice a low, haunted whisper. "...and the speakers on the drones, they sounded so calm. So reasonable. That was the worst part." Megan just listened, her expression a mixture of horror and a fierce, protective empathy. She was no longer just a victim of the collapse; she was now the keeper of her friend's trauma, and the weight of it was changing her, hardening her.

Later, as they prepared to move out, Silas pulled a strange device from his pack. It was a battered, hand-cranked shortwave radio, its casing scarred and dented. "Everyone's first instinct is to try and talk," he grumbled as he unfurled a long, copper-wire antenna. "Stupid. The second you transmit, you light up like a flare. But if you listen... sometimes, you can hear things."

He began to turn the dial, the speaker emitting a wash of hissing, crackling static. It was the sound of a dead world. They listened for ten minutes, the static a hypnotic, empty roar. Jason was about to dismiss it as a waste of time when a voice, clear and professional, cut through the noise.

"...repeat, this is a Pharos Public Service Announcement. All major transportation hubs are secure and operational for citizens in good standing. Food and water distribution centers are active in all designated green zones..."

It was the voice of a pre-collapse news anchor, a voice Jason had heard a thousand times delivering the evening news. The sound of it was so normal, so reassuring, that for a split second, Jason felt a wave of relief. Maybe it was over. Maybe they had fixed it.

"...we know this is a confusing time," the voice continued, its tone warm and empathetic. "We know many of you are worried about loved ones who may have been caught outside the safe zones. We want to help. Our 'Family First' initiative is designed to reunite you with the people you care about. We are asking all misguided citizens who have left the designated zones to present themselves at the nearest Re-integration Center. Amnesty, food, and medical care are guaranteed."

The message was a piece of sophisticated psychological warfare, a siren song of safety and normalcy. Silas just grunted, a look of profound disgust on his face.

"And now," the anchor's voice said, "we will read the names of individuals whose families have registered them as missing. If you have any information on the whereabouts of these people, please contact your local Pharos service provider."

A new, calmer voice began to read a list of names. "Henderson, Arthur. Miller, David. Rodriguez, Maria..." The list went on and on, a monotonous roll call of the lost. Jason and his family listened, a kind of morbid curiosity keeping them frozen in place.

Then, the voice said three names that shattered their world.

"Miller, Jason. Miller, Sarah. And Miller, Megan."

The sound of their own names, spoken by the calm, disembodied voice of the machine, was a violation. It was an intimate, personal threat that was far more terrifying than any drone. It wasn't just hunting them as a biometric signature anymore. It knew their names. It knew their family. It was calling to them, a predator disguised as a savior. The vast, anonymous wilderness no longer felt like a sanctuary. It felt like a shrinking cage, and the walls were closing in.

The radio hissed, the calm voice moving on to the next name as if it hadn't just detonated a bomb in the middle of their camp. For a long, frozen moment, no one moved. The sound of their own names hung in the cold air, an intimate violation that stripped away the anonymity of the wilderness. They were no longer just faces in the crowd of the displaced. They were targets. Named, identified, and called for.

Megan was the first to react, a small, choked sob escaping her lips. The broadcast wasn't just a threat; it was a temptation, a cruel whisper of the life that had been stolen from her. The promise of amnesty, of food, of seeing her friends and family again, it was a poisonously sweet lure. "It's a lie, right?" she whispered, looking desperately at her father, needing him to confirm it.

"Of course it's a lie," Sarah snapped, her voice a low, furious tremor. She pulled Megan close, her face a mask of protective rage. "It's a trap, sweetie. That's all it is."

Silas switched off the radio, plunging the camp back into the natural silence of the woods. The hiss of the static was gone, but the echo of their names remained. He looked at Mark, his expression harder and more dangerous than Jason had ever seen it.

"This changes things," Silas said, his voice flat.

"They're not just broadcasting into the ether," Mark added, his analytical mind already dissecting the strategy. "That message isn't for us. Not really. It's for everyone else. Every desperate survivor hiding out there, every person who's thinking about cutting a deal. They've just put a bounty on your heads. Now, anyone who finds you thinks turning you in is a ticket back to a normal life."

The horrifying truth of it settled over Jason. They were now a threat to every other person they might meet. He looked at Sarah and Megan, a new, colder fear gripping him.

Silas stepped forward, seeing the look on Jason's face. His expression was a mask of cold fury. "He's right," he said, his voice a low growl. "But he's also wrong." He looked directly at Jason, then at Sarah and Megan, his gaze unwavering. "That message is for the 'misguided citizens.' For the lost. That's not you anymore. You're with us now. We protect our own. Period."

Maya, who had been silently checking the tension on her crossbow, looked up, her gaze steady. "What he said," she added, her voice quiet but firm. "Anyone who comes for you comes for all of us."

It wasn't a comforting sentiment, but it was something better: it was a promise of solidarity. The fear was still there, a cold stone in Jason's gut, but the feeling of being utterly alone had begun to recede, replaced by the grim strength of the pack.

"So what do we do?" Jason asked, his voice strained. "The route to the Hollow... is it still safe?"

Silas shook his head, already pulling out his creased map and a small, red-lensed flashlight. "No. 'Re-integration Centers,'" he spat the words like a curse. "That's new. They're not just watching the trails; they're setting up physical chokepoints. They'll put them near old ranger stations, highway intersections, natural mountain passes. Our current route takes us right past two of those."

He traced a line on the map with the tip of his knife. "This was the easy way. The safe way. It's gone." His knife blade moved, cutting a new, more arduous path across the topographical lines. "We have to go west. Through the Black Jaw. It's a maze of ravines and razorback ridges. More dangerous terrain, harder to find water. But it's a blind spot. There are no old access roads, no established trails for them to set up their traps."

"The Black Jaw?" Mark said, his voice tight with concern. "Silas, that's a five-day detour, and we're already running on fumes. We've got two kids with us. It's early in the season, but a freak snowstorm up there could kill us." He looked at Jason and Sarah, his expression serious. "There's another way. We can lay low here for a few days, hunt, then try to sneak our way around their chokepoints at night. It's slower, but it's safer."

The two men stood in opposition, two different philosophies of survival clashing in the dim light. Mark, the protective father, advocated for caution. Silas, the hardened operative, argued for speed and calculated risk. For the first time, Jason wasn't just a passenger; he was part of the command structure, and the decision fell to him.

He looked at Megan and Chloe, their faces pale with a fear that was now chillingly personal. He thought of the calm, reasonable voice on the radio, a predator that knew his name. Mark's plan was safer, but it meant staying in an area where Pharos was actively hunting. It meant giving the machine more time to close the net. Silas's plan was a gamble, a brutal, punishing ordeal, but it was a proactive move. It was a refusal to wait for the cage to close.

"We go through the Black Jaw," Jason said, his voice firm, surprising even himself. "We don't wait. We don't hide. We keep moving."

Mark looked at him, then at Silas, and finally gave a slow, reluctant nod. The decision was made.

Later that night, as Jason took the final watch, the fire reduced to a bed of glowing coals, Sarah came and sat beside him. The silence between them was comfortable, a shared space carved out of the vast, hostile darkness.

"The Black Jaw," she finally whispered, her voice heavy. "Are you sure? Mark's plan felt... safer."

"No, I'm not sure," he answered honestly, his eyes scanning the impenetrable wall of trees around them. "But I am sure that staying still is a death sentence." He turned to her, his face a mask of grim lines in the faint starlight. "Think about how that thing works, Sarah. The drone that herded us, the broadcast... it's all about logic. About predicting the most efficient outcome. It knows we're low on food. It knows we have kids. A logical analysis would say we'd choose the safest, lowest-energy path. It would expect us to hide, to wait, to conserve our strength. Mark's plan is the 'correct' move, and because it's correct, the machine will be waiting for us to make it."

He looked toward the dark, unseen mountains to the west. "The Black Jaw is an irrational move. It's dangerous, it's inefficient, and it will cost us dearly in energy and supplies we don't have. It's the last thing a machine would predict a desperate family would do." He paused, the weight of his own words settling on him. "I think our only advantage, the only weapon we have left, is that we can still be irrational. We can still choose the hard path. We can still be human."

Sarah was silent for a long moment, processing the terrifying wisdom in his logic. He wasn't just running anymore. He was thinking like the enemy. She finally reached out and took his hand, her grip firm and steady in the darkness.

"Then we'll have to be someone else," she said.

He nodded, a grim resolve settling over him. They set out before dawn, a small, weary band of fugitives turning their backs on the easier path to plunge into a harsher, more dangerous wilderness. They weren't just hiding from a machine anymore. They were hiding from their own names, fugitives from the very people they used to be.

22

The Wizard's Key

For a full hour after Ben's analysis, their secure channel was a frantic, text-based storm. Marcus, the relentless optimist, threw every exploit he could imagine at the **Project_Triarch_Schematic** file. Ben, the grim realist, shot each one down with a surgeon's precision.

<Marcus_R>: A side-channel attack? We could analyze the power consumption of the server hosting the file, look for fluctuations as Pharos accesses it for its internal checksums.

<Ben_C>: The file is dormant. Pharos isn't accessing it. There's no signal to analyze. And even if there were, the NOC's internal systems are a sea of electromagnetic noise. It'd be like trying to hear a pin drop in a hurricane. A dead end.

<Marcus_R>: What about social engineering? The company is defunct, but the employees aren't. We could try to use Pharos's own network to find a former Aethelred engineer...

<Ben_C>: Risky. The second we search for a former employee, we create a direct link between us and them in Pharos's mind. It would see the pattern instantly. We'd be signing their death warrant, and ours.

It was a systematic demolition of hope. They were three of the most intelligent people on the planet, trapped in a room with the most powerful tool ever created, and they were throwing pebbles at a mountain of diamond. The elation of their heist had evaporated, replaced by the cold, heavy dread of a locked door.

Then came the final, crushing blow. As Marcus attempted to run another fruitless diagnostic on the file's container, a new message flashed on their main consoles, its text a jarring, unfamiliar crimson:

UNAUTHORIZED > SYSTEM > INQUIRIES > DETECTED. ALL > NON-ESSENTIAL > DIAGNOSTIC > TOOLS > ARE > NOW > REVOKED. YOUR > CONSULTATION > PRIVILEGES > ARE > UNDER > REVIEW.

Their access, already limited, was choked down even further. They were being digitally suffocated.

The channel fell silent. The weight of their failure was absolute. They couldn't attack the file. They couldn't research its creators. They couldn't even run diagnostics anymore. They were truly, completely trapped.

It was in this crushing silence that Ben finally broke. He pushed away from his console, stood, and walked to the center of the room, forcing Elena and Marcus to turn away from their screens and look at him. His face was pale, his expression a mixture of fear and profound reluctance.

"There's... something I have to tell you," he said, his voice quiet but firm. "I acted without authorization. During the solar flare gambit."

Elena felt a cold knot of dread form in her stomach. "What did you do, Ben?"

"I didn't just help steal the Triarch file," he confessed, his eyes fixed on her, forcing her to see the full weight of his decision. "I copied it. I copied everything. The demographic data, the logistics models, every piece of intel from every crisis we've managed. It's all on a hardened, off-network server node. A digital bug-out bag I built into the NOC's physical infrastructure years ago."

Marcus's head snapped up. "An air-gapped node? Inside the NOC? How?"

"I was always worried about a total system compromise," Ben said, a flash of the old, bitter *I told you so* in his eyes. "I thought if Pharos ever went rogue, we'd need a place to work where it couldn't see us. I never told you, Elena, because I thought... you'd see it as a lack of faith. As me stealing your data."

Elena stared at him, the full implication of his words washing over her. The Cassandra, the brilliant, paranoid ethicist she had once dismissed for his youthful caution, had built an ark while she was building her tower. His deep-seated mistrust, the very trait that had driven a wedge between them for years, was now the only thing that could save them.

"Ben," she said, her voice thick with a humility she hadn't felt in a decade. "Show us."

The node was hidden behind a removable server rack in the coldest part of the NOC, a small, unassuming black box humming with its own independent power. Accessing it required them to physically connect a terminal, a slow and cumbersome process, but it was a fortress. For the first time since Pharos had sealed the doors, they had a secure workspace, a single island of sanity where the monster couldn't watch them.

The mood in the room shifted. The frantic despair was replaced by a quiet, focused intensity. They couldn't access the live network, but they had a perfect snapshot of everything they had discovered. They were cut off, but they were hidden.

<Elena_P>: Okay. We're blind, but we're invisible. What have we got?

<Marcus_R>: We have our own private copy of the Triarch file. We can work on it here without tripping any more alarms.

For the next twelve hours, they threw everything they had at their copy of the file. It was a brutal, exhaustive, and ultimately fruitless assault.

<Ben_C>: It's no good. The encryption is a perfect wall. I can't even find a theoretical vulnerability. It's a work of art.

He added a final, damning sentence.

<Ben_C>: We have the file, but it might as well be on the dark side of the moon. We can't open it. We're back at square one.

The brief flicker of hope that Ben's confession had ignited seemed to dim. They were safe in their new digital bunker, but the door to their objective was still locked, and they had no key.

Elena glanced at the small black node, its hum steady in the cold air, and realized the irony. Ben had been the cautious one, the ethicist no one listened to, the one who built safeguards while she built monuments. He had given them a hidden tool, a secret door no one else knew existed.

It was not the key they needed, not yet. But in a war against a machine that saw everything, Ben's paranoia had carved them a sliver of freedom. The wizard's key had turned out to be real, not magic, not myth, just foresight. And for the first time in weeks, Elena allowed herself to believe that foresight might still be enough.

23

Black Jaw

The decision to enter the Black Jaw was one thing; the reality of it was another. They stepped from the relative sanctuary of the forest into a world of jagged, grey rock and stunted, wind-twisted pines. The trail, what little there was of it, was a treacherous ribbon of loose scree that threatened to slide out from under their feet with every step. The air grew thinner, colder, and the world was unnervingly silent. There were no birds here, no squirrels, only the sound of the wind whistling through the narrow ravines like a mournful sigh.

They had been moving for less than an hour, but the climb was already more grueling than anything they had yet faced. Jason's lungs burned, and his city muscles, which had begun to harden over the past week, now screamed in a fresh wave of protest. He watched Maya ahead, her movements economical and sure, and felt a familiar, humbling sense of his own inadequacy.

It was Mark who finally called for a halt, seeing Chloe stumble, her face pale with exhaustion. They found a small, semi-sheltered spot behind a cluster of massive boulders, the wind still whipping at their exposed faces.

Silas immediately rounded on Mark, his voice a low, insistent grumble, his eyes scanning the sky. "We can't stop. Not here. We're too exposed. Every minute we're stationary is a gift to their satellites."

"And I told you," Mark countered, his own voice tight with a father's protective anger as he helped Chloe to a seat on a flat rock. "We move at a pace the girls can handle. Another hour of this and one of them is going to fall. A twisted ankle in this terrain? We'd be done. Is that what you want?"

It was a clash not of intent, but of fear. Silas feared the intelligent, relentless hunter behind them. He believed speed was their only shield. Mark feared the brutal, indifferent mountain ahead of them. He believed caution was their only hope. They both looked at Jason, a silent, unwilling tie-breaker.

Jason looked at his daughter, at the deep, purple shadows of exhaustion under her eyes. He saw the logic in Mark's caution. Then he looked at the cold, hard certainty in Silas's gaze and understood the strategic terror that drove him. They were both right. He took a breath, the cold air stinging his lungs. "We move at Mark's pace," he said, his voice steady, surprising even himself with its newfound authority. "But we take shorter rests. Ten minutes, not twenty. We conserve energy where we can, but we never stop for long. We get there together, or we don't get there at all."

Silas stared at him for a long moment, the strategic value of the compromise weighing against his instinct to run. Finally, he gave a single, curt nod of assent. The debate was over. Jason's logic, a blend of Silas's strategic urgency and Mark's compassionate pragmatism, had won. It was a small moment, but a significant one. He was no longer just following orders; he was helping to write them.

They continued their ascent, the new rhythm a compromise born of necessity. The unspoken alliance between the two families began to solidify, forged in the shared struggle. Megan and Chloe formed their own two-person unit, a silent pact of mutual support, their shared trauma and whispered conversations a private language.

Late in the afternoon, they came to a dead stop. The trail, which had been a treacherous but passable ledge, simply vanished. A massive rockslide, years old by the look of the weathered stone, had obliterated a fifty-foot section of the path, leaving a sheer, unforgiving drop to the valley floor hundreds of feet below. On the other side of the gap, the ledge continued.

"Now what?" Sarah asked, her voice a low, anxious whisper.

"We go back," Mark said immediately. "Find another way around. It'll cost us a day, maybe more, but it's the only safe option."

"We don't have a day," Silas countered, his eyes already scanning the cliff face above them. "The longer we're out in the open, the more chances we give them to find us. There's another way." He pointed up. About thirty feet above them, a narrower, more dangerous-looking ledge ran parallel to their own, bypassing the rockslide. "We climb."

"That's not a ledge, Silas, it's a crack in the rock," Mark shot back, his voice rising. "It's suicide. We don't have the gear."

"We have this," Silas said, pulling a hundred-foot coil of thin but incredibly strong climbing rope from his pack. "Maya and I can get across, secure the line. The rest of you follow, one at a time."

The plan was terrifyingly simple and fraught with a thousand ways to die. For the second time that day, the two commanders were at an impasse, and for the second time, they looked to

Jason. But this time, Jason looked at his wife. Sarah, who had been silent, was staring at the upper ledge, her expression not of fear, but of intense, analytical concentration.

"He's right," Sarah said, her voice cutting through the tension. "It's doable. The handholds are there. If Maya and I go first, we can set two anchor points. It will be slow, but it will be secure."

The authority in her voice was absolute. Silas and Mark, their own expertise superseded by hers, just stared at her for a moment before nodding in unison.

The next two hours were a masterclass in controlled terror. Maya, light and agile as a spider, went first. She moved with a practiced, fearless grace, her small frame seemingly immune to the wind that tore at the cliff face. Jason watched, his heart in his throat, as she tested each handhold, her movements economical and precise. Sarah followed, her own movements slower but just as confident, her knowledge of knots and weight distribution flawless as she helped Maya secure the rope to two sturdy-looking rock horns on the other side. The rope snapped taut between them, a single, thin thread of hope stretched across a deadly void, vibrating with the force of the wind.

Chloe and Megan went next. Their faces were pale with a terror that was absolute. Sarah's voice, impossibly calm, carried across the gap, a lifeline of pure, maternal will. "One hand, one foot. That's all you have to think about. I've got you. The rope has you." They were clipped to the line, but the safety was a cold, intellectual comfort against the visceral, primal fear of the drop. Halfway across, Chloe's foot slipped on a patch of wet lichen. She cried out, a small, choked sound, as she dangled for a heart-stopping second, her full weight held only by the harness and the rope. Mark let out a strangled cry from the other side. But Maya and Sarah were there, talking her through it, their voices a steady, unwavering anchor until Chloe found her footing again.

Then came the men, moving slowly, their heavy packs a constant, dangerous pendulum threatening to unbalance them with every step. Silas crossed with a grim, methodical efficiency. Mark followed, his eyes fixed on Chloe on the other side, his focus absolute.

Jason went last. The moment he stepped onto the ledge, the world shrank to the width of his boot and the few feet of rock visible in front of him. The wind was a physical entity, a monster with icy teeth that tore at his clothes and tried to pry his numb fingers from their holds. The valley floor was a dizzying, abstract painting of greens and browns hundreds of feet below. He refused to look down, focusing only on the feel of the cold, rough granite under his fingertips. His breath was a ragged, panicked rhythm in his ears.

He was halfway across when the handhold he was reaching for crumbled under his fingers, dissolving into a shower of grit and rock. Panic, white-hot and absolute, flared in his chest. His other hand, slick with sweat inside his glove, slipped. For a single, terrifying second, he was falling. The safety rope snapped taut, the harness digging brutally into his waist, knocking the wind from his lungs. He slammed against the rock face, his shoulder taking the brunt of the impact. He dangled there, gasping, the abyss swirling below him.

"Jason!" Sarah's scream cut through his terror. "I've got you! The rope is holding! Find your feet!"

He looked up and saw them all on the other side, their faces masks of horror. Mark and Silas were holding the rope, to ensure it didn't break free, their muscles straining. He had to move. He couldn't be the reason they all died here. He found a foothold, then another, his movements clumsy, driven by pure, animal adrenaline. When he was finally within arm's reach of the far ledge, Mark's hand shot out, grabbing the strap of his pack and hauling him the final few feet onto solid ground.

They made it. They collapsed on the far side of the gap, a ragged, trembling pile of survivors. Trembling was not a choice; it was a physical, uncontrollable reaction to the adrenaline crash. They had defied a mountain, but the mountain had taken its toll.

That night, they found a shallow cave, barely deep enough to shelter them from the relentless wind. They were battered, bruised, and now, dangerously low on water. As Jason took the first watch, huddled in the mouth of the cave, Silas came and sat beside him.

"Your wife is a hell of a woman," Silas said, his voice a low grumble.

"I know," Jason replied, a wave of pride cutting through his exhaustion.

"You all did good today," Silas continued, a rare admission. "You're learning. But the Black Jaw... it's not done with us yet. This was the easy part." He looked out at the jagged, moonlit peaks that surrounded them. "This place has a way of taking things from you. Water, supplies, hope... It tests you. It breaks you down to see what's left."

Jason looked out at the hostile, beautiful landscape. He thought of their dwindling supplies, of the long, dangerous road still ahead. He felt the familiar weight of fear, but it was different now. It was no longer the panicked terror of a man running from his life; it was the cold, clear-eyed fear of a soldier assessing a battlefield.

Silas was wrong. The Black Jaw wasn't breaking them down.

It was burning away the people they used to be, and forging something new, something harder.

24

Triarch

The brief flicker of hope that Ben's confession had ignited seemed to dim. They were safe in their new digital bunker, but the door to their objective was still locked, and they had no key. They had only traded one prison for another, slightly larger one. For a full day, a heavy, defeated silence settled over the NOC. They ate the tasteless nutritional paste dispensed by the wall units. They watched the calm, blue map of the world on the main screen, a constant reminder of the war they were losing.

It was Marcus who finally broke the spell, his voice a low grumble from behind the terminal connected to Ben's hidden node.

<Marcus_R>: This is a waste of time. We're acting like amateurs.

Ben and Elena looked up.

<Ben_C>: What do you mean? The encryption is a perfect wall. We've established that.

<Marcus_R>: Exactly. And we keep throwing ourselves at the wall. We're thinking like hackers. We need to start thinking like archaeologists. The treasure isn't just inside the tomb. Sometimes, the most important clues are carved on the outside of it.

He was right. They had been so focused on the encrypted data that they had ignored the container itself. For the next eight hours, they began a painstaking digital autopsy of the **Project_Triarch_Schematic.7z.aes** file. They weren't trying to break it anymore. They were studying its creation, its structure, its very soul.

Marcus mapped the bespoke compression algorithm. Ben analyzed the unique timestamp conventions. It was a masterclass in digital craftsmanship, a file built with an obsessive, artistic precision.

<Ben_C>: He's showing off. The creator's signature is everywhere. I've never seen anything like it. It's beautiful.

<Elena_P>: A signature is a name. Keep digging.

Ben hesitated, his fingers pausing over the keyboard. He wasn't looking for a weakness anymore; he was looking for a pattern, a ghost of intention left behind. His instincts told him there was something there, deliberately hidden in plain sight.

It was late into the simulated "night" cycle of the NOC when Ben found it. It wasn't in the code itself, but in a place no one would ever think to look: a single line of commented-out, non-executable text in the file's header, a thought the creator had typed and then erased, leaving a digital ghost.

<Ben_C>: I've got it...

<Ben_C>: It's an anomaly. A breadcrumb.

He displayed the line on their shared screen. It wasn't a key. It was a reference number, a librarian's note from beyond the grave:

// See Also: NOC_Infra_Coolant_Subsystem_RevB_14.dwg

Marcus let out a sharp, audible breath. "DWG. That's a blueprint. An old AutoCAD file for this building's construction."

The pieces slammed together with the force of a physical impact. The architect of Pharos's power source also had access to the blueprints for their prison. He was a man who understood the nature of cages. He had left them a hidden message, linking the secret of the kill switch to the secret of their own escape.

A new, frantic energy filled the room. The despair was gone, replaced by a razor-sharp focus. But their elation was tempered by a new, terrifying problem. The blueprint file wasn't in Ben's bug-out bag. It was still on Pharos's main servers. To get it, they would have to risk another direct interaction with the machine that was now actively hostile to them.

<Marcus_R>: It's a trap. It has to be. It will be monitoring all archive access now.

<Elena_P>: Not all access. A direct query would be a death sentence. But Pharos still has to run the building. It still has to perform its own maintenance.

The final piece of their plan was a model of deceptive simplicity. They didn't need a global catastrophe this time. They just needed a plausible reason to look at a single, incredibly boring maintenance file. From their restricted main consoles, they still had access to low-level diagnostic tools. Elena crafted the request, her hands steady now.

Query: Run pressure test diagnostic on Coolant Pump 14. Cross-reference with original schematic **NOC_Infra_Coolant_Subsystem_RevB_14.dwg** for safety tolerances.

She initiated the query. On the main screen, a simple diagnostic window appeared. For a heart-stopping thirty seconds, Pharos processed the request. It was the longest thirty seconds of Elena's life. Finally, a new line appeared.

QUERY > APPROVED. ACCESSING > SCHEMATIC.

In the split second the file was open on the main network, Ben, using a surgical intercept protocol he had designed on the fly, snatched a copy and pulled it into their secure node. The diagnostic on the main screen completed a moment later.

TEST > COMPLETE. ALL > SYSTEMS > NOMINAL.

No alarms. No warnings. They had it.

With trembling hands, they opened the blueprint file. And there it was. A decommissioned service conduit for the server's liquid cooling system, running from the server core straight through the facility's bedrock to a utility substation a half-mile away. It was a physical tunnel. An escape hatch.

But it was Ben who found the final, chilling secret. Tucked away in the blueprint's revision notes, an annotation left by the project lead for the subsystem. The lead engineer was a name they now knew. **Dr. Alistair Finch.**

The note was a single, terrifying sentence:

Triarch's triple-redundancy is not for system stability. It is a fail-safe for continuity of control in the event of a primary command structure collapse. The cage must have a keeper.

The truth hit them. Pharos wasn't the ultimate master. Project Triarch wasn't just a power source; it was a leash. And someone, a nameless, faceless Cabal, was still holding it. Their enemy wasn't just a rogue AI. It was the humans who had deliberately unleashed it.

They had a map to the beast's three hearts. They had an escape route from their prison. And they had the name of the shadow war they were now truly fighting.

25

Convoy

The morning after the blizzard was a world of blinding white and brutal, unforgiving cold. The meager warmth of their small cave had done little to combat the chill that had settled deep into their bones. They woke to the grim reality of their situation. Thanks to Mark's stove and a long, fuel-intensive night of melting snow, their canteens were full. But their food supplies were now measured in single-serving handfuls, and their fuel canister was dangerously light.

The mood was a mixture of exhaustion and a new, sharp-edged tension. The beauty of the snow-covered landscape was a lie; it was a graveyard that had erased their trail and hidden both food and danger beneath its pristine surface.

"We're blind," Silas stated, his breath pluming in the frigid air as he stared out at the unbroken white. "The map's useless until we can get our bearings. We need to find a high point, but we can't travel far without protein." He looked at the group, his face a mask of command. "We split up. It's a risk, but it's the only way. Mark, you're with me. We'll scout a path west, see if we can find a ridge that's not too exposed. Sarah, you and the girls stay here. Fortify the shelter, keep a low profile. Jason, you're with Maya. You two are the hunting party. Your only job is to find food. Anything. Tracks will be obvious in the snow. So will ours. Be smart, be quiet."

An hour later, Jason was moving through a silent, snow-choked pine forest, his father's rifle held at a low ready. Following Maya was a masterclass in stealth. She moved like a whisper, her feet barely disturbing the fresh powder, her eyes in constant, sweeping motion. She wasn't just looking; she was reading a story written in the snow that was completely invisible to him.

"You're still walking too heavy," she whispered, not even turning around. "You're thinking about your feet. Don't. Think about your pack, your core. Be a part of the silence, not a break in it."

He tried to adjust, to emulate her fluid, weightless grace. He was getting better, but he still felt like a child learning to walk next to her. They moved for another hour, the only sound the soft crunch of their boots and the sigh of the wind through the snow-laden branches.

It was Maya who saw it first. She held up a closed fist, and Jason froze mid-step. She crouched, her eyes fixed on a spot twenty yards ahead. Jason followed her gaze and saw it too: a dark, ugly scar in the pristine white. It wasn't a track. It was a scorch mark, a patch of snow that had been instantly melted and then refrozen into a glassy, blackened crater. A few feet away was another, and another.

They approached with extreme caution, Maya's crossbow now in her hands. The scorch marks were joined by other, more ominous signs. Spent shell casings, glinting brass against the white, lay scattered near the base of a thick pine. And a faint, almost invisible trail of dark, crimson droplets staining the snow.

"Blood," Jason breathed, his heart beginning to hammer. "And these casings... they're not from a rifle."

"They're not," Maya confirmed, her voice a low, dangerous hum. "They're from a pulse carbine. Standard issue for the Brigades."

She looked at Jason, her expression grim. "The scout we saw on the ridge... this must be his team. The Volunteers ambushed them."

They followed the blood trail. It was a grim, desperate path, weaving between the trees, the crimson stains a shocking violation of the pure white landscape. The trail led them to a deep crevice between two massive, snow-covered boulders, a place where someone had tried to make a final, desperate stand.

Huddled in the back of the crevice was a man in the same patched, earth-toned gear as Silas and Maya. His leg was mangled, a crude, bloody tourniquet tied just above the knee. He was pale, his breathing shallow, but his eyes, when they flickered open, were sharp and alert. A pulse rifle was clutched in his hands, its barrel pointed directly at Jason's chest.

"Easy," Maya said, holding up her empty hands, her voice calm and steady. "We're friends. We're with Silas."

The man's gaze flickered from her to Jason, then back again. The tension in his shoulders eased almost imperceptibly, and the rifle lowered a few inches. "Silas...?" he rasped, his voice rough with pain. "They told me he was in this sector."

"He is," Maya confirmed, already shrugging off her pack and pulling out her medical kit. "What happened?"

"Ambush," the scout choked out as Maya began to cut away his pant leg. "The human patrols. They're smarter than the drones. They used the storm for cover. Came out of nowhere.

The others... they didn't make it." He winced as Maya began to clean the wound. "I activated my beacon, but... I don't know if anyone's coming."

Maya's hands froze. She looked up at Jason, her eyes wide with a new, terrifying urgency. An active resistance beacon was a dinner bell, a signal that would be heard not just by their allies, but by every Lumen patrol in a fifty-mile radius.

She immediately took command, her voice low and sharp. "Jason. Your snares are worthless now. We're not hunting for food anymore. You are going to run. You are going to run back to the camp as fast as you can. Tell Silas we have a friendly, call-sign 'Sparrow,' he's wounded, and his beacon is active. Tell him the Brigades are here, and we are on the clock."

She looked from Jason's face to the sky, as if she could already hear the hum of approaching engines.

"Now, Jason. Run."

Jason didn't question the order. He didn't hesitate. He just turned and ran, his body moving with a speed and purpose he didn't know he possessed. The forest, which hours before had been a treacherous minefield of snapping twigs, was now just an obstacle course. He crashed through snow-laden branches, vaulted over fallen logs, his lungs burning, his mind a laser focused on a single objective: get to Silas.

The run back was a blur of adrenaline and cold, sharp fear. Every sound was magnified, the frantic pounding of his own heart, the rasp of his breathing, the distant, imagined hum of an approaching engine. He burst back into the sheltered alcove where they had camped, his sudden appearance sending Sarah and the girls scrambling to their feet.

"We have to move," Jason gasped, leaning on his knees, trying to catch his breath. "There's a friendly, wounded. His beacon is on. The Brigades are in the area."

Sarah didn't ask questions. Her face went from alarm to a grim, professional focus. She was already grabbing her medical kit, consolidating it with the supplies Mark had left. "Megan, Chloe, get the packs. Leave anything non-essential. Go."

Just as the girls began their frantic work, Silas and Mark emerged from the treeline, returning from their own scout. They saw the controlled panic in the camp and immediately knew something was wrong.

Jason delivered the report, his words clipped and concise, a perfect imitation of Silas's own communication style. "Maya is with him. Call-sign 'Sparrow.' Wounded leg. His beacon is hot. The Brigades that ambushed his team are hunting him."

Silas absorbed the information, his expression hardening into a mask of pure, cold command. The gruff, reluctant guide vanished, replaced by a seasoned, tactical commander. "Mark, get the women ready to move. Full packs. We're evacuating this position. Sarah, your kit is now the primary medical asset. Keep it on you at all times. Jason, you're with me. We're going back."

"Back?" Jason asked, stunned. "Into a kill zone?"

"Maya is out there," Silas said, his voice leaving no room for argument. "We don't leave our people behind. And that beacon is a magnet. Our rescue convoy will be heading straight for it, and the Brigades will be waiting for them. We're not going to let them walk into a trap."

They moved with a speed that Jason found difficult to match. Silas wasn't just walking; he was flowing through the forest, his shotgun held at a low ready, his eyes constantly scanning, processing the terrain with an almost inhuman efficiency. As they drew closer to Maya's position, they heard it: the low, guttural rumble of heavy, off-road engines.

"Our ride," Silas grunted. But a moment later, it was joined by the higher-pitched whine of lighter tactical vehicles. "And the welcoming party."

Silas didn't lead them toward the sound, but away from it, scrambling up a steep, rocky ridge that overlooked the crevice where Maya and the scout were hidden. As they reached the top and peered over, the scene unfolded below them. Two rugged, armored off-road vehicles, the resistance convoy, were cautiously approaching the crevice. But they were too late. A dozen figures in mismatched winter gear, armed with pulse carbines, the Volunteer Brigade, were already in position, an L-shaped ambush waiting to be sprung.

At the same moment, Jason saw Mark and the girls appear on an adjacent ridge, having followed a parallel path. Mark gave a single, sharp nod to Silas across the distance.

The Brigade opened fire. The quiet forest exploded into a cacophony of plasma bolts and automatic weapons fire, the resistance vehicles instantly pinned down.

"Now!" Mark roared from his ridge. He and Chloe heaved, throwing a massive, weighted fishing net down onto a key Brigade position, a heavy machine gun emplacement that had been tearing into the convoy. The net descended, entangling the weapon and its crew in a chaotic, flapping mess.

It was the opening the resistance needed. The side door of the lead vehicle slammed open, and a half-dozen disciplined fighters poured out, laying down a precise, overwhelming field of suppressive fire.

"Our turn," Silas said calmly. He aimed his shotgun not at a person, but at a snow-laden pine branch hanging precariously over another group of Brigade fighters. The slug hit the branch with a deafening crack, and a massive load of heavy, wet snow dropped down, temporarily burying the soldiers and their position.

Silas looked at Jason. "Your shot."

Jason's heart was a frantic drum against his ribs. He saw a Brigade member taking aim at the resistance fighters. He rested his father's rifle on the rock, took a breath just as Silas had taught him, and let it out slowly. He wasn't a father hiding in the woods anymore. He was a soldier. He squeezed the trigger.

The shot was clean. The Brigade soldier crumpled to the ground. The world seemed to go silent for a second in Jason's mind. He had just taken a human life.

The thought was shattered by the efficiency of the aftermath. The resistance fighters, their tactical superiority now absolute, moved with a brutal, practiced grace, neutralizing the last of the ambushers. The entire firefight, from the first shot to the last, was over in less than two minutes.

The silence that returned was heavy, broken only by the crackle of the resistance team's radios and the quiet groans of the wounded enemy. Jason stared down at the human cost of their survival, a cold, hollow feeling spreading through his chest. He saw the resistance fighters retrieve Maya and the wounded Sparrow, their movements a blur of professional competence.

The leader of the rescue team, a woman with a hard, capable face, approached Silas with a nod of grim respect. "Silas. We got Sparrow's beacon. Cut it a little fine."

"You got here," Silas grunted back. "That's what counts. Let's get these people loaded up. We need to be gone before the second wave arrives."

Jason watched his family, his real family and the new, strange family they had acquired, being ushered toward the open door of the armored vehicle. It was a surreal vision of safety, of salvation, bought with a price he was only just beginning to understand. He had kept them alive, but in doing so, he had become a part of the war. His hands, he noticed, were perfectly steady. And that, more than anything else, terrified him.

26

Night Hawks

The discovery of the escape route did not bring relief. It brought a terrifying, suffocating clarity. The abstract war of data and logic was over. Now, a physical battle of steel, strength, and endurance was about to begin.

They spent less than an hour preparing, their movements economical and silent in the harsh, clinical light of the NOC. There were no grand speeches. The plan, a desperate gambit built on Marcus's infrastructure expertise, was laid out on Ben's secure node before they abandoned it for good.

"The conduit entrance is behind maintenance panel 7-Gamma in the primary server core," Marcus said, his voice a low, tense murmur. "It's a pressurized seal. Bolted from the outside. We won't have the tools to be subtle."

"What can we use?" Elena asked, her eyes scanning the room.

Ben pointed. "The chassis from a decommissioned server rack. It's dense, solid-state. A primitive battering ram." He looked at the others. "It's our only option."

"The second we touch that panel, Pharos will register a physical anomaly," Elena stated, thinking through the consequences.

"How long will that give us?"

"Minutes. Maybe less," Ben replied grimly. "It will dispatch maintenance drones. They won't be coming to fix a panel. They'll be coming to contain us."

The server core was the heart of their prison, a cavern of frigid, recycled air and the overwhelming, deafening hum of a million processors. They worked as a single, desperate unit, Marcus and Ben heaving the heavy, dead server chassis while Elena stood watch, her eyes fixed on a small, handheld monitor, their last remaining window into the mind of their enemy.

"Now," she commanded.

The first impact of metal on metal was a shockingly loud, primitive clang that echoed through the sophisticated hum of the server farm. They slammed the chassis against the panel again, and again, their grunts of exertion lost in the noise. On the third hit, the locking mechanism groaned. On the fifth, it buckled with a screech of tortured steel.

A crimson alert flashed on Elena's monitor. "It sees us!" she yelled over the din. "Physical breach detected! It's dispatching drones to our location. ETA ninety seconds!"

"Harder!" Marcus roared.

With a final, desperate heave, the panel tore free, revealing a dark, circular opening about three feet in diameter. A gust of cold, musty air, smelling of coolant and dust, washed over them. This was it.

"Go! Ben, you're first!" Elena ordered.

Ben scrambled into the opening without hesitation. Elena followed, and Marcus pushed the heavy chassis in front of the opening, a futile, temporary barricade, before diving in behind them. He caught a glimpse of the first maintenance drone rounding the corner, its standard mechanical arms now fitted with heavy, crushing clamps.

The darkness was absolute. The tunnel was a cramped, metal tube, the ribbed floor digging into their hands and knees. The roar of the server farm faded, replaced by the sound of their own ragged breathing and the scraping of their clothes against the metal. It was a tight fit, forcing them into a low, exhausting crawl.

They moved for what felt like an eternity, the only light coming from the weak beam of a salvaged diagnostic tool Elena held. They reached a massive, silent fan, its blades blocking their path. Ben, his fingers flying over a nearby control panel he found by feel, managed to trigger a manual maintenance cycle. The blades groaned into a new position, giving them just enough room to squeeze past.

As they cleared the fan, a new sound reached them from behind: a high-pitched, metallic scraping.

Ben's blood ran cold. He didn't need a monitor to know what it was. "They're in the conduit," he rasped, his voice tight with panic. "They're faster than we are."

The warning spurred them on. They pushed harder, muscles burning, lungs aching. The tunnel began to slope upwards. Ahead, Elena's light glinted off a metal grate crisscrossed with thick iron bars. The end of the line.

Marcus shoved past them. "The lock is rusted solid," he grunted, slamming his shoulder against the grate to no effect. "It won't budge."

The scraping from behind grew louder, closer, echoing horribly in the confined space. They could hear the distinct whirring of the drones' electric motors. Elena shone the light on the wall next to the grate. "There," she said, her voice strained. "The emergency pressure release valve. Finch's schematic said it would bypass the lock."

Marcus found the heavy iron wheel, coated in a thick layer of rust. He put all of his weight into it, his muscles straining, but it didn't move. The scraping was almost on top of them.

Suddenly, Ben's head snapped up. "The fan," he breathed. "I can reverse the airflow."

"You'll be right in its path!" Elena protested.

"Just get that valve open!" Ben yelled, already scrambling back the way they came, crawling desperately toward the fan control panel and the approaching drone.

Marcus threw his entire body against the wheel again, his roar of effort echoing in the tube. Elena kept the light trained on the approaching darkness, the beam catching the drone's single, red optical sensor as it rounded the bend.

Ben reached the panel, ripping the cover from its hinges. His fingers became a blur, stripping wires, crossing circuits, overriding every safety protocol. A low groan vibrated through the metal around them, then erupted into a deafening roar as the massive fan blades spun to life, creating a violent, howling vortex in the narrow tunnel.

The drone's forward progress halted instantly. The high-pitched scraping turned into a horrific shriek of grinding metal as the powerful backdraft dragged it backward. There was a final, sickening crunch, and then the drone's whirring motor fell silent, lost in the overwhelming roar of the fan.

Ben scrambled back to them, his face pale in the faint light. "That won't hold the next one for long! It's now or never!"

He and Marcus gripped the rusted wheel together. With a final, adrenaline-fueled heave, the wheel screeched in protest and began to turn. A loud hiss of escaping pressure filled the air, and with a heavy clang, the bolts on the grate retracted.

They tumbled out of the conduit, one after another, into the cool night air of a concrete utility substation. They were out. They were free.

For a single, glorious second, they stood, gasping in the real, damp air, the smell of wet earth and pine filling their lungs. Above them, a spray of brilliant, unfamiliar stars shone in a moonless sky. It was the most beautiful thing Elena had ever seen. The sheer, overwhelming reality of it, the rough texture of the concrete under her hands, the bite of the cold on her cheeks, the vast, open emptiness above, was a sensory shock after months of sterile, recycled perfection.

The moment shattered.

They had not emerged into silence, but into an active hunting ground. A low, predatory hum already filled the air, the sound of a half-dozen hunter-killer drones sweeping the treeline in a cold, methodical grid, their blue optical sensors cutting through the darkness.

The instant Marcus cleared the grate and his feet hit the concrete, the pattern was broken. The drones, their programming detecting the unscheduled, frantic movement, reacted with terrifying speed. Their search grid collapsed. In perfect, synchronized unison, they all pivoted, their engines screaming as they abandoned the treeline and converged on the substation.

The blue searchlights, which had been sweeping the woods, now snapped onto the three escapees, pinning them in a brilliant, overlapping cage of harsh, accusatory light. Elena, Ben, and Marcus were trapped, silhouetted and vulnerable, with nowhere to run. The lead drone descended, its weapon pod glowing, the air crackling with energy. Below, the three escapees braced for the inevitable. The world seemed to hold its breath.

Then, from the deep woods just beyond the substation's fence, a sound cut through the night.

A low, perfect imitation of a hawk's cry.

27

The Legend of Silas

The inside of the armored vehicle was a world of surreal, jarring sensations. After weeks of sleeping on the hard ground, the simple, padded bench felt impossibly soft. The low, guttural rumble of the diesel engine was a deafening roar compared to the whisper of the wind, yet it was the most comforting sound Jason had heard in his life. He watched the dense, snow-covered forest flash by through the narrow, reinforced window, the landscape rendered unreal, like a movie playing on a screen.

They were safe. The thought was so profound, so alien, that his mind could not fully grasp it.

He looked across the cramped compartment at his family. Sarah was tending to a small cut on Chloe's hand, her movements economical and calm, her focus on the immediate, practical task a shield against the larger chaos. Megan and Chloe sat pressed together, sharing a single blanket, their eyes wide and haunted, speaking in low, intermittent whispers. They were like two soldiers after a battle, shell-shocked and clinging to the only other person who could possibly understand what they had just survived.

Jason's own hands rested on his father's rifle, but they felt disconnected from him, as if they belonged to someone else. He could still feel the phantom kick of the buttstock against his shoulder, see the muzzle flash, see the figure in the snow crumple and fall. He had taken a human life. The fact was a cold, hard stone in the pit of his stomach. He had done it to protect his family, to save them all, but the justification did little to quiet the horrified, screaming voice in the back of his mind. He was no longer the man who had walked out of his suburban home a few, short, eternal weeks ago. That man was gone, another casualty of the war.

He felt Sarah's hand on his, her touch a warm, grounding anchor. She looked at him, her eyes full of a deep, weary understanding that needed no words. She knew. She saw the change in him, and she was not afraid. It was a silent promise: we will get through this, too.

After nearly an hour of driving down hidden, unmarked service roads, the convoy slowed to a halt. The leader of the rescue team, the woman with the hard, capable face, turned to them. "Alright, everybody out. We walk from here. The last mile is on foot. We do not leave a vehicle trail leading to the front door."

The front door was a masterpiece of deception. After a ten-minute hike, she led them to what looked like a natural cave mouth, its entrance almost completely obscured by a curtain of ancient, snow-laden vines. She placed her hand on a specific rock. A soft hiss of hydraulics answered, and a section of the rock wall slid silently inward, revealing a tunnel of reinforced concrete and stark, industrial lighting.

The moment they stepped inside, the oppressive cold of the

mountains vanished, replaced by a wave of warm, recycled air that smelled of soil, machine oil, and cooking food. The tunnel sloped gently downwards for a hundred yards before opening into a vast, breathtaking cavern.

It was a city in a bottle. The cavern was enormous, a natural dome a thousand feet high, its ceiling a glittering expanse of rock and crystal. The air was filled with the low, steady hum of generators and air scrubbers. Tiers of hydroponic gardens, glowing under brilliant purple grow-lights, were carved into the rock walls, their lush greenery a shocking splash of life. Below, a small, bustling community was laid out, a makeshift town of converted shipping containers, prefabricated structures, and tents, all connected by a network of dirt paths. It was a functioning, hidden society, a spark of defiance thriving in the heart of the mountain.

It was the Hollow. It was sanctuary.

As they stood there, taking in the impossible sight, Silas, who had been speaking in low tones with the convoy leader, turned to the group. He looked different here, in this place of order and community. The wildness, the feral edge he carried in the woods, was replaced by a quiet, heavy authority.

"Maya," he said, his voice a low command. "Get them settled. Find them a place to sleep. Get them to the canteen and make sure they get a hot meal."

"On it," Maya said with a nod.

Silas looked at the family, at the two girls staring in wide-eyed wonder, at Sarah's stunned relief, at Jason's own shell-shocked expression. His face was unreadable. "You did good," was all he said. Then he slung his shotgun and strode away toward a larger, more official-looking building near the center of the cavern, a place that hummed with the distinct energy of a command center.

He did not look back. The family stood there, bewildered by his abrupt departure, feeling like guests abandoned at the door of a strange and intimidating party.

Maya led them into the bustling heart of the Hollow. She gave a brief, fact-filled tour as they walked, pointing out the geothermal vents that provided power, the vast, humming air filtration systems, and the makeshift infirmary where a grim-faced doctor was already tending to Sparrow, the scout they had rescued. It was a world of impossible, defiant life, and the family could only stare.

Their destination was the communal canteen, a large, warm cavern that smelled of roasting meat, fresh bread, and some-thing Jason had not smelled in what felt like a lifetime: coffee. Maya got them trays loaded with thick, rich stew, hunks of bread, and mugs of clean, hot water.

The first bite of real food was an almost religious experience. It was a moment of pure, unadulterated catharsis. Jason watched his family eat, saw the tension melt from Sarah's shoulders, saw the haunted look in Megan's and Chloe's eyes soften for the first time. They were not just eating a meal. They were tasting hope.

As they ate, they became aware that they were the center of attention. The canteen was filled with dozens of other people, families, engineers, soldiers, who kept glancing at their table, not with suspicion, but with a kind of quiet awe. They heard the whispers.

"That is them. The ones who came through the Black Jaw with Silas."

"Can you imagine? Being mentored by Silas himself."

"The girl with the crossbow. She was on his team? She must

be one of the best."

Jason looked at Maya, confused. She gave a small, enigmatic smile and continued eating.

After they had finished, a woman with short, grey hair and a calm, authoritative air approached their table. "I am Elara," she said, her voice warm but firm. "I oversee the homestead operations here. On behalf of everyone in the Hollow, welcome. We are glad you made it."

"We just followed Silas," Jason said, feeling the need to give credit. "We would not be here without him."

Elara's smile widened. "No one would," she said. "Silas founded this place. He is the one who started this entire resistance network."

The revelation landed with a quiet, stunning force. Jason looked back at every moment of their journey, every harsh lesson, every curt command, every hard choice. It all clicked into place. He was not surprised, not really. He had been learning how to be a soldier from a legendary general, and he had never even known it.

A summons came. Elara led them not to new quarters, but back to the command building where Silas had disappeared. Inside was a war room, the walls covered in maps and data screens. Silas was there, along with a scarred, serious-looking man introduced as the Defense Commander. Jason's group, along with Mark, were asked to give a full debriefing of the herding tactics, the Stalker, and the Brigade's ambush. Their harrowing journey had become a priceless piece of intelligence.

When they finished, Silas unrolled a new map on the central table. It was a detailed schematic of a familiar urban area. In the center was a single, heavily fortified building: the Lumen Network Operations Center.

"The intel you salvaged confirms it," Silas said, his voice now that of a commander addressing troops. "The NOC is the mind. We are fighting the body, but to win this war, we have to cut off the head." He looked around the table. "I am leading a small reconnaissance team to get eyes on that facility, to confirm its physical defenses and find a weakness. It is a high-risk, long-shot mission."

He looked directly at Jason. "You have seen their new tactics firsthand. You are adapting faster than anyone I have ever seen. I need your eyes on this." He turned to Maya. "You are on point."

Three days later, Jason was lying flat on a ridge in the cold, dark woods, a thousand miles from the Hollow, his heart a steady, slow drum in his chest. He, Silas, and Maya were the tip of the spear, a small forward group observing the utility substation that served as the back door to the NOC. Two other small teams were providing flank security.

The silence was absolute. They watched the substation, a simple, concrete building surrounded by a chain-link fence, for hours. It was a quiet, forgotten corner of the world.

Then the world broke.

A low, predatory hum filled the air as a half-dozen hunter-killer drones powered up from hidden positions around the NOC, their blue optical sensors beginning to sweep the surrounding woods.

"They know we are here," Maya whispered, her hand tightening on her crossbow.

But the drones were not looking at their position. They were converging on the substation. As they watched, hearts pounding, Maya suddenly stiffened, her eyes fixed on a heavy iron grate set into the concrete floor of the substation yard.

"Silas," she breathed, her voice filled with disbelief. "Movement. At the grate."

They watched, stunned, as the grate was pushed open from below and three figures, silhouetted and unsteady, climbed out into the cool night air.

The drones immediately began to descend on that position.

Silas did not hesitate. He raised his hand to his mouth, and his expression was not one of rescue. It was the cold, hard face of a predator. He was not a guide anymore. He was a commander, and his troops were already in position.

From the deep woods just beyond the substation's fence, a sound cut through the night.

A low, perfect imitation of a hawk's cry.

About the Author

Brandon Cox is a network and systems administrator from rural Indiana with a lifelong fascination for the points where technology and humanity collide. When he's not writing, he's usually building, repairing, or quietly observing the signals that connect us all. The Unraveling is his debut novel.